DEADLY GAMES

ELUSIVE KILLERS
BOOK ONE

ALEXIS KENNEDY

Library of Congress Control Number: 2018951081

Title Wave Publishing LLC
Union, MO
http://bit.do/AlexisKennedy
Cover design by Xcite! DesignZ
edited by BB Editing

BOOKS BY ALEXIS KENNEDY

Bound Through Blood

Under the Blood Moon (Hearts on Fire Book 1)

Ravaged (Dial M for Murder Book 1)

Déjà Vu (Dial M for Murder Book 2)

Cupid (Dial M for Murder Book 3)

Two Faced

Scandalous

Angry House

Birthright

Indelible (Two Faced book 2)

Gods and Angels

Lycan Moon (Hearts on Fire Book 2)

Deadly Games (Elusive Killers Book 1)

Every story has a voice, so let it speak to you.
                                    ~Alexis Kennedy

CHAPTER 1

June 20, 2016
St. Louis, MO

I WOKE UP early Monday morning for my first day in St. Louis County Police Department's Homicide Unit. After working for seven years in Vice and the Drug Unit, I finally got to move up when Detective Robert Haas retired.

My face hurt from smiling as I walked down the crowded corridors, trying to make a good first impression. I knocked on Lieutenant Daniel Madden's door and stepped inside when he waved to me through the glass pane.

"Good morning, Lieutenant Madden," I greeted him.

"Good morning, Sasha. Let's go introduce you to the rest of the unit."

He led the way into the bullpen where desks were jammed up against each other in the cramped space. I saw one empty desk and assumed it was now mine.

"All, I want you to meet Detective Sasha Delossa. I snagged her from the Drug Unit to fill our vacancy. I'm sure you will catch her up on open cases and make her feel welcome."

A tall bald man stepped forward and thrust his hand toward me. "I'm Sergeant Detective Liam Davis. Welcome to the team."

"Thank you, Sir," I replied, but he scowled.

"No need for formality in this unit. You can just call me Liam."

I nodded and shook hands with the others as they introduced themselves. I met Eric Riley and the only other female in the unit—Marisol Kendall. My desk was butted against Marisol's, and when I sat down in the office chair, I smelled the heavy stench of cologne.

Marisol obviously recognized the look of distaste because she told me, "I know. He liked to splash it on in the morning."

I pulled out a container of Lysol wipes from my box of belongings and wiped the desk and chair down. It helped some. Once I got my drawers unstuck from the duct tape they'd jokingly put on them, I was ready to dive in.

"What do I need to look at first?" I asked Liam, and he handed me a short stack of file folders.

"These can use a fresh pair of eyes, so give them a scan first. We'll go from there."

I nodded in understanding and cracked open the first folder. It was a case on a drive-by shooting of a seventeen-year-old female on Biddle Street in Carr Square. According to her grandmother, she'd been on her way to the Lorretta Hall Park to meet friends in the early afternoon of May 7th. Her friends called the house when she never showed up, claiming they'd heard gunshots. The young woman, Latoya Lamarre, was an honor student with a promising future, but she had the misfortune of living in a bad neighborhood ran by the Crips.

That got me to thinking about my confidential informant from my days in the Drug Unit. My CI, Maria Gomez, was known to associate with the various Crips and Bloods, but the rival gangs didn't know about it, or she'd already be dead. I put in a call to her.

After telling her I was now a part of the Homicide Unit, I asked about the shooting. "Have you heard anything about it from your *friends*?"

"Nah, I ain't heard nothing about it. I'll keep my ears open for you though, chica. Say…um…does being your CI for homicides and shit pay more? I mean, that's harder work on my end with all these boys up in here and their turf wars."

I smiled to myself. She sure tried hard to wheedle every dime I had. "I'm sure we can work something out, Maria. You call me if you find anything out. It was May 7th near Lorretta Hall Park," I reiterated.

"I'll get back to ya if I hear something," she replied and then screamed at someone talking loudly near her. "I'm on the damn phone!"

"It's okay, Maria. I've got to go, but you call me if anything comes up." I hung up and stuck my finger inside my ringing ear.

"CI, huh?" Marisol asked. "I could hear her from over here."

I laughed. "Yep, she's a loud one. She runs around with the Crips and Bloods, kind of alternating between them. She's helped me on drug busts, so she's valuable to SLCPD."

Marisol shrugged. "We take whatever help we can get in this department. The more eyes and ears we have out there, the better."

I nodded and thumbed through the file again, reading the interviews conducted in the case. I didn't get very far, though, when Liam addressed us all.

"There's been a body found in Forest Park, outside by the Boathouse's dumpster. The woman is too mangled for a positive ID, so we'll have to wait for dental records, but Tamara Boyd was reported missing last night by her fiancée. He claims she was headed to the zoo yesterday to meet her sister, Dominique Boyd, but she never arrived. Search dogs found the body."

Marisol raised her brows at me. "Welcome to Homicide. There's no time like the present to break you in." She rose from her desk and strapped on her Glock. "You can ride with me."

I followed them to the elevators, feeling woozy from the sudden excitement. It was like going on a drug bust, but it was worse since someone had died. More than ever, it made me want to uphold my badge.

CHAPTER 2

WHEN WE ARRIVED on the scene, there were two patrol cars still there, but the SLCPD Canine Unit was pulling out. I love dogs, and I had been fortunate to work with some of the canines while in the Drug Unit.

"Are you ready for this?" Marisol asked, and my pulse raced even faster.

"I believe so. I've always wanted to join the Homicide Unit, so I'm excited. Isn't that morbid?" I wondered.

She laughed, "I guess it is a little, but then it applies to us all. Someone has to die for us to get paid."

She parked next to the other cruisers, and we jumped out to join our team. When we approached the body, I could smell the metallic scent of a horrid death from several feet away, and it burned my nose. I'd smelled decomposing bodies before, but this was different than a drug overdose. This was the scent of someone's suffering and pain.

Eric noticed me cringing and said, "You'll get used to it before you know it."

I grimaced at him. "That's what I'm afraid of. How do you get used to murder?"

He sighed, "Sadly, by the constant exposure."

The crime scene was a drastic contrast to the serenity of Post Dispatch Lake. Thankfully, the restaurant wasn't open yet, and the lake area was void of fishermen. There were plenty of lookie-loos driving down Government Drive, though. The sound of screeching tires bounced off the building as the drivers slammed on the brakes to rubberneck. The less-interested drivers furiously honked their horns and tried to pull around.

"All we need is a car wreck out here on top of this mess," I mumbled under my breath.

The distorted body was splayed on the ground in front of the dumpster. She had on slashed remains of a tank top and shorts, which were soaked with blood. The M.E., Chris Edwards, was hunched over her.

He glanced up with a look of disgust and announced, "Based on her liver temperature, she's been dead for about four hours. She has multiple stab wounds and lacerations all over her body"—he turned her head toward us—"including her face."

"And she wasn't carrying ID, right?" Marisol asked him.

Sam Conner, who was one of the officers still on the scene, spoke up. "No, we didn't find a purse or ID on her or in the dumpster."

"This looks personal," I observed, and they all looked in my direction. "It's overkill, to say the least, and why slash her face?"

"Keep going," Liam encouraged, "What else do you see?"

I looked at the ground, not enjoying being put on the spot, but I was grateful I had the chance to prove my worth to the team.

"Well, there isn't enough blood here, so she's been moved from the primary crime scene. Also, the killer is likely male because it would take strength to move a woman of her size, and statistically speaking, women don't normally mutilate other women. It's usually a misogynistic male"—I looked back up at Liam—"How did I do?"

They all smiled, and he praised my efforts. "I think you made a sound and thorough assessment, especially for a first attempt."

I felt a blush creep up my neck and into my cheeks. "Thank you. I've done a considerable amount of reading, including FBI manuals."

Eric barked with laughter. "It's your first day in the Homicide Unit, and you're already thinking about leaving us for the FBI?"

I shook my head with a giggle. "No, I just like to know what I'm dealing with is all."

Marisol clasped my shoulder with a light squeeze. "That's a good attitude, and it will help you thrive in this unit."

Dr. Edwards stood and told us, "I'm going to take her back to the morgue and begin the autopsy. I'll let you know when my report is finished and when I have her identity confirmed." He waved for his techs to remove her remains.

Liam cleared his throat. "As Sasha pointed out, we need to find the primary crime scene, and of course, we need to start interviews. Let's get the sister and fiancé in as soon as possible."

When we returned to SLCPD, I sat in on the interview with Tamara Boyd's fiancé, John Washington.

The distraught man had apparently been waiting at the station all morning.

"Did you find her?" he asked as soon as Marisol and I entered the interview room.

"We're not sure, Mr. Washington," Marisol began. "Can you tell us what she was wearing the last time you saw her?"

Through his tears, he sobbed, "She had on a red blouse and a black skirt."

I shared a knowing glance with Marisol. It didn't match our victim's clothes. "Are you sure that's what she had on when she left your house?" I asked, and he nodded.

"Why? What do you know?" he questioned us with narrowed eyes. "What aren't you telling me?"

I quickly answered him, "We aren't keeping anything from you because we don't know anything for sure yet. I don't want to upset you further until we know something definitive."

His hands were shaking, and tears streamed down his face. He sobbed, "I heard some officers talking, and they said there was a-a-a body. Oh god! Is it her?"

Marisol answered him this time. "We don't know yet. We're waiting on dental records. Does she have any tattoos or birthmarks on her body that might help us?"

He nodded rapidly. "She has our son's name inked on her right wrist. It's Jayden."

"Thank you for the information. Now, if you'd like to remain here, you can certainly do so, but if you want to go home and rest, we'll contact you as soon as we know something," Marisol informed him.

He stood up so abruptly that his metal folding chair toppled over and clanged to the floor. Instinctively, my hand flew to my Glock, but I didn't withdraw it.

Marisol tried talking to him again in a more soothing tone as he anxiously paced the room. "We're going to go check on some things, but you can stay here and wait."

He slumped back into a chair and put his face in his hands to cry. He wasn't going anywhere, so I closed the door behind us to give him some privacy.

"When is the sister coming in?" I wondered.

Marisol pressed the down button for the elevator and tossed a sideways glance at me. "Not until we know whom we have in the morgue. It doesn't appear to be her, though."

I couldn't argue with that. "I guess we'll find out soon enough," I mumbled as we stepped onto the elevator.

CHAPTER 3

HE WALKED IN circles around the fetching woman, who was bound to the wooden beam. He made a tsking sound repetitiously and stared into her terrified eyes without blinking once. He studied her expression—or what he could see of it since duct tape was across her mouth, and a muscle in his jaw twitched as he envisioned all he would do to her.

When her eyes went blank, as if she was trying to disassociate herself from her circumstances, he squeezed her shoulder hard enough to leave a deep bruise.

"Look at me!" he demanded sharply. "I need to see what you're feeling." Tears puddled in her widened brown eyes, and he responded with laughter. "See now? That's much better. That's helpful." But he wanted more.

He peeled back the tape from her mouth to see her full red lips. She bit into her lower lip while sobs escaped her.

"Why are you doing this?" she begged.

He picked up a camera and directed her, "That's it. Show me how you feel. This is the stage, and you are the star. I want to see what you're thinking." *Click. Click.* "Perfect. Now let's see what this does for your mood." He held up a large butcher knife, and shrill screams filled the dank concrete room.

"Help me! Someone, please help me!" she cried at the top of her lungs while he continued to snap photos.

"Let it out," he laughed maniacally. "No one can hear you." He set the camera on a tripod set up in front of her and grabbed the remote switch. "It's time for a close-up," he growled and stepped closer to her.

"Please don't hurt me. Just let me go, and I'll forget all about this," she pleaded. Her entire face was distorted with terror, and he just kept taking pictures. He also kept stepping closer with the knife.

"Do you know what the director says when the scene is finished?" he taunted with an evil smirk. "He says cut."

He drew the tip of the knife down the length of her left forearm, bound above her head to the beam, and blood streamed down her body to puddle on the floor.

Her screams sounded melodious to him. *Why have I waited so long to try this?*

CHAPTER 4

THE MORGUE WAS cold and smelled of disinfectant and death. Chris looked up from the mutilated body with a grim expression, but no one would expect anything less.

"I don't have the DNA or dental comparisons back just yet, but I did put a rush on them," he informed us.

"Can you see if she has the name Jayden tattooed on her right wrist?" Marisol asked him.

He gestured to her arm and explained, "She doesn't have any tattoos or identifying birthmarks on her at all. I already checked."

"What about sexual assault?" I asked, and he shook his head.

"No, there was no evidence of trauma, and I did a swab to check for necrophilia, but it came up empty," he replied, and the idea made me cringe. "I didn't find prints or foreign hairs on her for trace either. He was very careful."

I got to thinking about something I'd read in an FBI forensics manual. "Killers who use knives usually cut themselves in the process, so did you swab for foreign blood cells?"

He smiled. "I'm glad you know that, and yes, I collected swabs. The crime lab is processing them."

Marisol had been staring at the body, but she finally looked up at me. "Well, let's go tell Mr. Washington the good news. Since this isn't Tamara Boyd, she could still be alive."

I nodded in agreement. "Okay. I'm wondering if maybe she got cold feet about the wedding and just took off on her own."

She frowned and nodded. "I hope that's the case. I truly do."

John Washington's twisted face relaxed, and a gush of air escaped his mouth. "I'm so glad that it isn't her, but where can she be?"

I gently asked him, "Mr. Washington, is there a chance she just needed a few days to herself, so she went somewhere? Is it possible that she has cold feet about your wedding?"

He slammed his fist on the table, causing our folders to displace. "No! She waited three years for me to propose, and when I did, she started making all the plans. We're supposed to get married in three months, and she's been nothing but excited about it. She has her dress, the catering, the flowers, and the cake all taken care of already"—he put his head in his hands and sobbed—"Jayden is going to be the ring bearer, and she loves him more than anything in this world, so I know she didn't just take off."

"I understand," I calmly assured him. "We'll notify the Missing Persons Division to keep looking for her. Is there any place she may have stopped off at before meeting her sister at the zoo?"

The distraught man wiped his wet eyes. "I don't know. You'll be better off to ask Dominique about that. She only told me about the zoo."

I thanked him for his time and told him we'd be in touch once we found anything out. He agreed to go home to his son and wait for our call.

I spoke to Jamie Tinsley in Missing Persons and told him to question the sister and to get the search dogs back out in Forest Park. When I got back to my desk, Liam was on the phone with the M.E. When he hung up, he rubbed his hand over his jaw and told us something we didn't want to hear.

"The identity of our victim has been established. She's Larissa Ray from Shrewsbury, and she was reported missing by her husband two weeks ago. Chris says she had an empty digestive tract, and she exhibited signs of malnourishment. Some of the cuts are older than others, and there's also burn marks on the soles of her feet. Cause of death is exsanguination. However long this jackoff had her, he was putting her through torture."

Marisol raised an eyebrow at me. "Still glad you joined us?"

I leveled my gaze at her and slowly nodded. "Yeah. I want to catch this bastard."

CHAPTER 5

HE FLAUNTED HIS superiority in front of the broken woman, pacing in circles around her like a lion circling a wounded elk. She continued to beg for her life, but it fell on deaf ears, not that he would kill her *now*. No, he needed time with his new plaything before she became disposable. He needed time to fully understand her suffering.

He took another drag on the cigarette before blowing out rings that stretched around her, making her cough.

"I know. It's a nasty habit, isn't it?" He spoke to her like they were old friends. "I really should quit or pick up a new vice." He sank down in front of her and lifted her quivering foot off the cold floor. "Do you know what my father did to me when I was a child?"

"No," she sobbed almost too quietly for him to hear.

"When I was bad, which I guess was fairly often, my father, the chain-smoker, would use me as his ashtray. Here, let me show you." He put the cigarette out on the bottom of her foot, and her cries of pain made him smile with narcissistic pleasure. He set her foot back down and rose to face her. "I learned to cope with the pain, though. In fact, I learned to *use* it." He reached for a cup of water and thrust the straw toward her trembling lips. "Take a drink." She obeyed and took several gulps before he pulled the cup away from her. "That will have to do for now. I don't have supper for two."

He sat down at a small table he had set up in front of her and began to eat his steaming meal of pork chops, potatoes, corn, and rolls. When he was finished, he threw the bone at her feet.

"Here, this is for you," he said with a malicious smile followed by laughter. "Enjoy."

Of course, there was no meat on the bone, and her arms were still bound above her head, so it didn't matter anyway.

"I can't sleep if you're screaming all night, so I'm afraid I'll have to tape your mouth again," he whispered and reached for the roll of duct tape.

"No, please don't. I promise I'll be good. I promise you won't hear a peep," she begged.

He wagged his finger in front of her nose. "Tsk-tsk. I don't know you that well yet, so I don't trust you."

He tore off a large piece and covered her twisted mouth. Then he took one more photo of the rage, fear, and despise in her eyes before shutting off the light and heading up to bed.

CHAPTER 6

I GLANCED AT my watch; it was already 8:30. After the long day we had, I was exhausted, but I knew I wouldn't fall asleep if I went to bed. The new case was haunting me, and I had the feeling the horror was just beginning.

I was sitting on my couch and flipping through my collection of criminology books when my cell phone suddenly rang and made me jump. I looked at the display and saw that it was my recent ex-boyfriend, Justin. We'd broken up during my last undercover assignment for the Drug Unit. He hated the constant danger the job brought and its crazy hours, and I hated that he wanted to control me. I let his call go to voicemail. He's the assistant district attorney, so chances are we'll cross paths professionally again, but I didn't have to deal with him right now. I went back to my reading and brushed up on famous serial killers, wishing I had a large dog to cuddle with and make me feel safer. I had an alarm system and my Glock, but I needed a companion, and now that I wouldn't be going undercover anymore, I would finally have the time for one. I knew just the one to adopt. My neighbor was about to be deployed and was worried about what to do with his Belgian Malinois, Duke. I gave him a quick call and told him I'd love to have the large dog.

"That's great because I deploy in three days, and I still don't have a home for him. He's a good boy, but no one wants a dog this big," Dave explained.

"Well I do, and I'll take excellent care of him," I promised.

"I'm sure you will, and congratulations on the promotion," he gushed. "You can pick him up tomorrow if you want. Separating from him is going to be hard on me, so I might as well get it over with. You can have all his toys, bedding, food, etcetera."

"Great. I'll stop by after work if that's okay," I suggested, and he agreed.

After we finished talking, I felt relaxed enough to go to bed. Unfortunately, I had disturbing dreams all night long.

I got to work thirty minutes early on Tuesday to go back over my notes on the current case.

"You're early this morning," Lieutenant Madden remarked as he walked past my desk. "Is everything okay?"

I looked up from the file. "Yes, I'm just going back over everything from yesterday. We need to crack down on this before anyone else suffers."

He rocked back on his heels. "So, you don't think this is a case of one and done?"

"No, I don't think so. I think he's just getting warmed up. Larissa Ray was gone for two weeks, and the restaurant was just a dump site, so he kept her somewhere for the torture. You don't behave that sadistically if it's for just one person," I theorized. "I think he's either had the obsession for a while, or he's just starting out with it."

He rapped his knuckles on my desk. "I concur. Good job."

I heard the elevator doors slide open, and the others stepped into the office all at once. Marisol handed me a coffee from Starbucks.

"I think you'll like that better than the diesel fuel they serve around here," she joked.

I yawned and replied, "Thank you. I was up late, so I need the extra boost."

Eric had overheard us and asked me, "First-day stress kept you up? Well, don't worry because we all went through those sleepless nights too."

"*Went through?* I still have those nights, and last night was no exception," Marisol remarked. "I had to watch my favorite movie to relax."

"What's your favorite movie?" I wondered, expecting her to say something along the lines of a Disney movie.

"*Jaws,*" she replied, and I almost spit my coffee out all over my desk.

Once they were settled in, we discussed the case and bounced ideas off each other. I told them the same thing I'd told the lieutenant, and they liked where I was leading.

"Just to play the devil's advocate, what if it was just a personal vendetta against Larissa Ray, and Tamara Boyd's disappearance is a coincidence?" Liam asked us.

"Then why leave the body where it would be discovered?" I challenged. "He could've dumped her in the lake or buried her if he was just getting revenge." I paced the area between us while the wheels turned in my brain. "Larissa Ray wasn't a high-risk victim. She lived in a good neighborhood with her husband and worked as an administrative assistant." I paused so they could react and interject with their own ideas.

The lieutenant interrupted, though. "I just received a call from the patrol commander. A student found a body on the SLU campus. Units and the M.E. are already en route."

We were headed for the elevator before he could say anything else.

CHAPTER 7

WHEN WE ARRIVED on the scene, the patrol officers had the courtyard taped off. The bright yellow crime scene tape mocked the peacefulness of the grassy quad. Curious students and faculty were crowded around it to get their stares in before heading off to class.

We waded through the crowd, and I cringed in horror at the display on the other side of the tape. The young male was even more mangled than Larissa Ray. In addition to the knife wounds, his hands and legs were facing unnatural directions, indicating broken bones. I wanted to look away, but I couldn't; this was the job now.

I noticed something sticking out of his shirt pocket. "What's that?" I asked and pointed to it for the M.E.

Chris removed the object, which was a horrific photo of Larissa Ray. She was bound to a beam, and her bulging eyes broadcasted her panic. I put on latex gloves and stuffed the photo inside an evidence bag before handing it over to a member of the CSU team.

"He's proud of himself," I mumbled. "He's telling us he's just getting started with this."

Liam heard me and replied, "He has a grandiose sense of self-importance, and now we know he has no gender or race preference."

Chris looked up and told us the victim, who wasn't wearing any ID, had likely died of exsanguination as well. "He's also cold to the touch, so I think he might have been in cold storage. That will make it hard to determine the time of death."

I rubbed my temples. This was looking worse than we thought. If the killer was storing the bodies, he could have been killing for a long time.

"We're going to need to try to find a connection between the victims," I mentioned. "But I'm sure you already knew that," I added softly, realizing that I was the one new at this, not them.

Eric nudged my shoulder. "We did, but I'm glad you also know it. Additionally, we need to see how long he's been missing after he's identified."

Chris released the body to his morgue techs and the crime scene to the CSU techs, and we headed back to the station.

The message light on my desk phone was flashing when I got back, so I dialed in to retrieve my voicemail. I had a message from Jamie Tinsley.

I got in touch with Dominique Boyd, and she said her sister didn't mention any stops before meeting her at the zoo yesterday. Let me know if you need anything else.

I told the others, and they looked just as frustrated as I felt. We were getting nowhere fast. I called Jamie back and asked if they had any leads on Tamara Boyd.

"No. The search dogs didn't find anything, so divers are checking the lakes around Forest Park, but with as many lakes as there are…"

"It will take some time to check them all," I finished for him. "Although, assuming she is a victim of the same perp, he's all about leaving his victims out in the open so far, and he's keeping them long enough to torture them. The first victim had been held for two weeks, and we don't know about the man we have in the morgue yet."

"So, she might still be alive then," he concluded. "Hopefully, you'll get to her in time, and I'll let you know about the new victim as soon as I hear from the crime lab. I'm already running reports on local males reported missing in the last month who fit his profile."

"Good idea. Stay in touch." I hung up and relayed his information to the others.

I was engrossed in my notes when my cell phone rang. It was Maria Gomez.

"Maria, I'm glad you called. Did you find anything out for me on that young lady?" I inquired while flipping through the files on my desk for the one in question. I was focused on the current case, but I was determined not to let the older one slip by. "It would sure make my day."

She lowered her voice, so I knew she wasn't alone. "Yeah, I got something, but I can't tell you right now. Can you meet me?"

I looked at my watch: it was 11:00 already. "Sure, where are you?"

"I'm at a friend's house on the corner of Jefferson and Market," she answered quietly.

"I can meet you at the Market Street Deli, and I'll buy you some lunch, okay?"

"Sure. I'll be there in ten minutes," she responded and hung up.

I looked at the others and told them, "I need to run a quick errand regarding this other case from last month"—I held up the file folder—"but I'll be right back."

Liam nodded in approval. "That's fine. We're just waiting on Chris to do the autopsy and for lab reports, so we'll call you if we need you back right away."

I quickly took the stairs to the first floor and ran to my car in the parking garage. I couldn't wait to bring scum to justice—even if it wasn't the worst scum out there doing harm right now.

CHAPTER 8

WHEN I ARRIVED at the Market Street Deli, I saw Maria standing outside, fidgeting nervously and puffing on a cigarette. As soon as she saw me, she snubbed out the cigarette with her shoe and walked inside the shop. She didn't want to be seen walking in with me, which was smart given whom she spent time with.

I gestured to a corner that was away from the windows, and she strutted over to sit down. I ordered two turkey sandwiches with sodas and sat at the table behind her, so our backs were to each other and we could talk over our shoulders. I handed her a sandwich, and she wasted no time before digging into it. I think she spent more money on booze and cigarettes than she ever did food.

She leaned back and whispered, "So, I found out something about your girl. The day she was walking to the park, Carlos Garcia was riding around the neighborhood, looking to start trouble."

I knew the hoodlum she was talking about. He was a member of the Bloods, and he always pulled an alibi out of his ass when it was on the line. He was too high up on their food chain not to have someone always covering for him and taking the fall. I would love to be the person who finally got the charges to stick.

In between bites of my sandwich, I asked, "Was he alone or with his crew?"

She shook her head and mumbled with a full mouth, "Alone."

"Any witnesses?" I wondered and jotted down some notes. "I mean, how did you find out about this?"

She took a drink of her soda and nervously glanced toward the windows. "Because I overheard Fernando bragging to his old lady about it. He said he and Demarcus rolled up on Carlos, and he threatened to pop them like he"—she lowered her voice and made air quotes—"'had just done some black bitch.'"

"That's good, but I'm going to need more than hearsay to make charges stick," I told her solemnly.

"Well, I figured you would want to hear it for yourself, so I recorded the conversation with my phone"— she handed her cell phone over with the voice recording app opened—"Get it off there if you don't mind."

I emailed the recording to myself and deleted it from her phone. "Okay, I deleted it after sending it to myself."

"Is that enough to put him away?" she wondered.

I bit my bottom lip. "While recordings aren't admissible in a court of law, it should be enough to get a warrant to search his car and home for the gun. Then we just have to match the ballistics up."

"So I did good, right?"

I slipped her a twenty-dollar bill. "You did very well, Maria. Now if you can help with this current case, that'd be remarkable."

She turned around to face me this time. "Do you mean the one in the news about the bodies that were just found?"

I nodded with a frown. I felt the tension mounting in my neck from just thinking about it.

"Well, I'll see if I can find anything out for you," she offered. "But I don't think the Crips or Bloods are involved. It ain't their style, you know?"

"Yes, I know. There might be more than one doer, but it's not gang-related. I'd bet good money on it," I stated. I wasn't aware of any gangs that were as vicious or organized as this killer. "Anyway, I need to return to the station, so you stay out of trouble and get in touch with me if you hear or see anything."

She held her fist up for a bump. "I will. Keep it real, five-o."

"You too, Maria," I replied and left with the rest of my sandwich, consuming it on the way back to the station.

I felt some relief. At least I could get somewhere with this case, but I had to do it before the weekend, which was coming up. Even judges would be off, making it hard to get a search warrant.

When I got back to the station, I explained to the others, who were still waiting on the M.E. and crime lab reports, what had happened and opened the email I had sent to myself. We all listened to it, including Lieutenant Madden, and they all agreed it was enough to request the search warrant.

"Judge Holkem is normally good about getting warrants to us quickly, so call his office first," the lieutenant commanded. "But if he's not available, try Judge Shapiro."

I got right on it and was able to get the warrant from Judge Holkem. The reports came in on the current case, though, so we had to tend to that first.

Chris brought all the reports up to us from the autopsy and crime lab. The man's prints weren't in AFIS, but his DNA was in CODIS because he was reported missing on March 12th by his parents. He was twenty-year-old Tucker Brown from Webster Groves. He was working as a car mechanic for Ray Unnerstall at Ray's Garage and Used Cars in Webster Groves and had failed to show up or call into work. After a couple days, Mr. Unnerstall called his home and notified his parents, who'd just assumed he was gallivanting around with his girlfriend, Janine Barber, but she'd not heard from him either, so they filed the missing person's report and used his toothbrush to collect the DNA sample.

"I'll go downstairs and send uniforms to Webster Groves to notify the family and assure them that we are going to be working on this," Marisol offered and took the parents' address information with her.

While she did that, the rest of us began going over the autopsy results with Chris. "He died from internal bleeding, but he suffered major organ damage, sustaining stab wounds to his kidneys and liver. I'm surprised his heart didn't give out from shock—it would've been the better way to die. He wasn't sodomized, but he was tortured. He has burns on his soles, and as you saw at the body dump, he has broken wrists and legs too. Just like with the first victim, the slashes were made over a period of time, and he was starved. He suffered a world of pain"—he rubbed his temples—"I just can't imagine someone being this sadistic."

"Could he have been in cold storage for very long?" I asked. "He's been missing for over two months."

He nodded. "He could have been in storage for several weeks."

"I'm going to see where large coolers or meat lockers can be bought around here and if any had been sold in the last two months," Eric offered.

I paced the area between our clusters of desks and thought aloud. "Larissa Ray wasn't in storage, so he must have taken the full two weeks with her and then dumped her when he took Tamara Boyd, assuming he did. But where and how is he getting them, why dump them so far apart, and of course, what is his motive?"

"That's where our job comes in," Liam stated. "We need to find the connection. We know he has no gender, race, or economic preference, so what is his end game?"

But where do we even look?

CHAPTER 9

TEARS STREAMED DOWN her face, and she felt like her legs were rubber. They kept trying to give out, but with her arms restrained above her head, she had to try to stand, or she risked breaking her wrists against the cuffs binding them. She shook from hunger pains, and her head spun as she repeated silent prayers. Her mouth was still taped, and her throat burned from screaming into it. She was thankful that at least he hadn't raped her. The thought of his vile touch made her dry heave against the tape, and only stomach juice came up. She had no idea what time it was or what day it was. The windows were blocked by shrubs and only let in a crack of light. She heard dripping from somewhere and used the noise to count off minutes until her eyelids were too heavy to keep open. She knew she was going to die. She just hoped it would be over soon.

The door at the top of the stairs opened with a loud creak that pierced the quiet, and her heart thudded in her chest. Maybe he'd kill her now. Maybe he'd give her the sweet relief she longed for. His heavy footsteps down the groaning stairs echoed off the concrete walls and made the slash in her arm burn worse. She supposed if the blade had gone deeper, she would've bled out. She'd be okay with that at this point. It was just a matter of time. If no one heard her screams yesterday, or whenever it was, then no one was coming to save her. She was alone in her hell, and the despair was crushing her heart and soul.

He loved the look of defeat in her dull eyes. "Did you miss me?" he cackled. "I'm guessing you want some of this refreshing cold water"—he held up a bottle of Aquafina—"I'm sure you're a little thirsty by now."

She nodded with what little strength she had left in her neck.

"This might sting a little," he sneered and ripped the tape off her mouth with one quick and hard yank.

She cried out from the pain and the relief. It was so good to take a deep breath again. She accepted a drink from the cold bottle, sucking the refreshment down her scalding throat. He only gave her two pulls before yanking it away, though.

"Not too much. I wouldn't want you to get sick," he sneered and scooted an empty bucket underneath her. "In case you have to pee."

"Please…my arms and legs hurt so bad. Please let me down," she begged. "I won't tell anyone if you let me go. I promise not to tell."

He chuckled, and the sinister sound made her shake more than she already was. It was a clear *no*.

"I think you know I can't do that yet, but I promise to let you go eventually. I'm just not done with enjoying your company," he ground out with a malevolent smile. He picked up a knife from his table, and the small crack of light coming down the stairs glinted off it, making it even more threatening. "I'm not going to lie to you; this is going to hurt."

"No, dammit!" she screeched. "If you want to kill me, just kill me and get it over with!"

He wagged his finger at her like he was berating a child. "Ah-ah-ah...we'll be done when I say we're done. Now smile for the camera." *Click. Click.* He snapped her picture and then raked the tip of the knife down her other forearm while snapping a close-up of her terrified, pain-filled screams.

He stood back and flipped through the photos on the digital camera. Something was missing. He needed more terror, more pain.

"Tsk-tsk...I don't think these will do. Something is lacking on your end, my muse. You need to try harder," he sniped and approached her.

He marred her face this time with a scalpel. He began underneath her left eye and made an arc to her chin. Then he stepped back to admire his work. He liked the pain and rage in her eyes, so he took more snapshots. Then he finished off the water bottle and used it to collect her dripping blood.

"I think this will do for tonight, but I'll be back down if not. Rest well. Tomorrow is going to be a big day for you," he threatened and climbed back up the stairs.

He got into his car and drove to his second location. He had someone else to check on.

CHAPTER 10

WE HAD SPENT all afternoon going over the details of the case and rereading the reports on the victims. The only thing they had in common with each other was that they had crossed paths with a merciless son-of-a-bitch. Serial killers always had something that linked their victims, so what were we missing?

We called it a day at 5:30, even though we were still stumped, and I was on my way home. When I pulled into my driveway, I realized I needed to go next door to get Duke yet. I put my purse and gun inside the house and then trotted over to Dave's and rang the bell. Duke barked ferociously until he saw it was me.

"Tough day?" Dave asked when he saw my drawn expression.

"Tough case," I moaned and rubbed the back of my neck. "I'm sure you've seen the news."

He let me step inside the house, and Duke sat down in front of me and pawed my leg. I sat on the couch and petted him while looking into his big brown eyes.

"Yes, I saw the news, and it's just awful. It's hard to imagine something that horrible in our backyards, even with the high crime rate around here," he replied. "Do you have any suspects at all?"

I swung my head. "Not a one. Nothing ties the cases together so far, but of course, I'm not allowed to discuss the details of an ongoing investigation either."

"I understand. Well, I have all of Duke's things together for you"—he picked up a large cardboard box— "It's heavy, so I'll carry it over for you."

I rose from the couch and snapped the dog's leash on him. "Okay, buddy, let's go to your new home."

As soon as I opened my front door and unhooked the leash, Duke took off running through my small single-floor house to thoroughly sniff everything.

"He looks like he's going to be fine," Dave chuckled. "And I'm leaving tomorrow. I'm heading to the Airforce base in Virginia for a day before deployment."

I laughed as Duke buzzed by us again. "I promise to love and care for him dearly. You don't have anything to worry about with him but take care of yourself over there. Do you know how long you'll be gone?"

He stretched his arms behind his head and sighed. "I'm going to do my best to be careful. They said to anticipate being gone at least a year, but they said that last time, too, and I was gone for over two years. I got Duke when I returned home because I didn't expect to be sent back over, and he helped me with the PTSD."

Duke stopped running and stood protectively by Dave's side. I tossed some of his toys around the living room to make it look more like home to him, and he watched me curiously.

"I have all of his vet paperwork in the box too. He's three years old, and he's up-to-date with his shots and whatnot," Dave told me before bending down to hug his dog goodbye. "You be a good boy for your new mom. I'm really going to miss you. When I get back, we'll hang out sometime, okay?" He held his hand up, and Duke tapped it with his paw. "High-five...good boy."

I gave him a hug and wished him well again before he left. In another time, he would have made a great catch for me.

Duke whimpered and planted himself in front of the door after Dave left, so I attempted to distract him with his toys. He played for a minute, but he lacked interest for the most part. It broke my heart to see him sad.

I put leftover roast with veggies in the microwave for my supper while I filled his bowls with food and water. I gave him some of the cold roast I still had left on top of his food to help him relax.

"You can't bribe an officer, but I can certainly try to bribe you," I cooed and scratched him between the ears while he chowed down.

After dinner, I cleaned the kitchen up while he played with a squeaky toy in the living room. Then I played tug of war with him, using his rope toy, and naturally, he won. I glanced at my watch and saw that it was already 8:00, so I ran a hot bath. He lay on the bath mat, whining softly for his dad, while I soaked. After everything I'd seen in the last two days, it felt good to have the large dog there even though he was sad.

I double-checked the alarm and doors after his last potty and then climbed into bed. Luckily, I had a fenced yard for him to go out in, and I decided to get a dog door installed as soon as I could to allow him to go out during the day. He curled up on the floor, but I patted the bed until he jumped up and lay next to me.

"That's a good boy," I said soothingly. "Give me cuddles."

I closed my eyes, thinking my dreams wouldn't be as bad tonight, especially since I didn't do any heavy reading before bed.

CHAPTER 11

I HEARD ON the local news that there was a wreck on Lindell Boulevard, so I left early to take an alternate route to work. Unfortunately, everyone else had the same idea, so Grand Boulevard was a sea of red brake lights and honking horns. I was five minutes late by the time I reached the third floor at SLCPD.

"Sorry that I'm late. There was a wreck, and going around it wasn't easy," I mumbled to Liam.

He smiled and assured me, "You're not the only one. Marisol and Eric aren't here yet."

"Maybe I should've used my siren," I joked, and he chuckled with me. "Any news on the case?"

He looked up from the papers he had retrieved from the fax machine, and tension was pooled in his eyes. "Possibly so," he mumbled and sank into his chair. "This is from downstairs. Some blood was found in the parking lot of the Fox Theater, and it matched in CODIS to a missing man from Kirkwood. Thirty-year-old Andrew Adams was reported missing four days ago by his wife, Jane, when he didn't come home after work. He works in

Kirkwood at a butcher shop, and no one there has heard from him either."

Marisol and Eric rounded the corner, and they were both out of breath. "The elevator was on the top floor, so we took the stairs," she explained and noticed our grim expressions. "What did we miss? You two look like someone stole your puppy."

Liam told them everything he'd just told me, and we put our heads together, going over the facts we had so far. Our killer had no preferences showing yet. He didn't care about race, gender, or economic status. He was a sadist, and he appeared to be sticking to the St. Louis region, which likely meant he lived in it.

"He's not leaving trace evidence, so he has some degree of education, possibly in forensics. The torture suggests that he kills for pleasure, and it might indicate ties to organized crime, but I don't think that's the case. He's likely white and between twenty-five to forty years old," I suggested, based on the months of profiling research I'd completed to get the job when it was close to becoming available.

They all stared at me, and I felt self-conscious as if I'd said something stupid. I crossed my legs and waited for the critique to begin.

"I think that's a solid assessment," Liam stated. "I can see you learned a lot before joining us, and that's good. It will help with this case."

I felt myself blush harder, and I wanted to fan my face. "Thank you. I appreciate your feedback. Now, how do we put it to use, and when can we do the search on Carlos Garcia's crib?"

He tapped his pen on his notepad. "Let me answer the second question first. You and Eric can go search his place now. I want you to partner with each of us to learn the dynamic. I'll stay here with Marisol and work on this Slasher case."

"Slasher case, huh? Is that what we're going to call it?" Marisol inquired with a smirk.

"Do you have a better name?" he wondered, and she shook her head.

Eric gestured for me to follow him, so I grabbed the search warrant off my desk as well as my notepad, Glock, and the file folder. It wasn't my first time serving a warrant, but it was my first murder investigation, and I was chomping at the bit to bring in Garcia.

Considering Garcia ran with the Bloods, Eric had three patrol cars go with us to help keep the peace. Several men and women scattered as soon as we rolled up on his address, but he stood on the porch with his arms over his chest. He was always so cocky, and I desperately wanted to wipe the smug smile off his scarred face. A few of his boys stayed behind and puffed out their chests as a threat.

"Wassup, pigs? Why you be rollin' up in my face?" Carlos asked.

I showed him the search warrant. "We're going to take a look around your place and your ride"—I turned to the uniforms nearby—"You two search the Impala, and you two keep an eye on him," I directed them, and they nodded in affirmation.

Eric patted him down while two uniforms patted his lackeys down. They were both packing heat, and the weapons were quickly confiscated.

"Whoa there," Carlos exclaimed. "You can't take those. Those belong to us for protection."

I smiled smugly at him. "Actually we can since that's what we're looking for, and I'm sure you don't have licenses for conceal and carry. They belong to the evidence department at SLCPD now."

He grumbled something incoherent and took a seat by his homies.

I followed Eric into the dump Carlos called home. It was a run-down two-story clapboard that had to be at least sixty years old. I knew from previous dealings that his grandmother had left it to him in her will. It smelled like a mixture of booze, cigarettes, sweat, urine, and garbage. I had to cover my mouth with my shirt to keep from gagging, and it looked like Eric was having the same trouble.

We rummaged through the first floor while two uniforms went upstairs to search. There was a lot of junk to dig through, and I tried to put myself in his shoes. *Where would I hide a gun with at least one body on it?* I checked in the toilet tank, under the mattresses, and tapped on the walls for hollow hiding spots. They were the same places druggies liked to hide their stashes.

Eric checked the floorboards for any loose ones and the ratty furniture for hidden pockets. Sure enough, under the floorboard, we found some drug paraphernalia and a 9mm with the serial number filed off. I tucked the gun inside my waistband and bagged the drug-related items, which included a crack pipe and about two ounces of cocaine.

Just in case there were more guns, we kept looking through the rat hole. In the kitchen, I found another 9mm on top of a cabinet, and then the uniformed officers came down the stairs with several grams of heroin.

"We didn't find any weapons, but we found this beauty," Officer Taniya Ames stated with a smirk.

Eric looked at me in surprise. "Didn't the Drug Unit have its eye on him at some point?"

"Yeah, they always watch the gangs. We brought him in a few times, but someone always took the fall and did his time for him. That's why I need to tie him to the murder weapon. I'm tired of seeing this piece of shit walk," I replied.

After the basement was checked, we were done sweeping the house, and the officers checking his car were finished as well. They hadn't found anything.

"That's okay because we're bringing them in anyway for these," I told them and held up the guns and drugs.

"Those aren't mine," Carlos yelped. "They belong to my homies, man."

"Tell it to the judge," I snapped and cuffed him.

The items immediately went to the crime lab for testing, and the ballistics on the gun that was under the floorboard matched to the bullet pulled from Latoya Lamarre. Additionally, it had Carlos Garcia's prints all over it. His DNA was on the crack pipe, so we had him for that, too. I finally got the bastard, and he'd be going away for a long time.

I volunteered to go tell Latoya's grandmother the terrific news.

"Oh my heavens, thank you! I'm so relieved you caught the scum responsible," she cried in relief. "I'm so glad you all didn't forget about my poor Toya.

"We're happy to be of service, Ma'am," I assured her and then headed back to the station and the nightmare case we were working on.

CHAPTER 12

HE LOOKED AT the man with his wrists and ankles chained to the wall and felt smug. The man was bigger and stronger than him, but he'd broken him down into a pile of sobbing nothingness.

He took several photos of the man's grief, and that gave him another idea. It was pure genius.

"Why are you doing this to me?" the man sniveled through tears and blood-filled slobber. "What do you want? I have money, and you can have it if you just let me go."

He laughed at his victim. "I don't want money. I want to see your pain."

He set the camera up on the tripod and grabbed the baseball bat from the table. He took a hard swing at the man's right knee, hearing the bones splinter into tiny shards while one large piece ripped through the flesh. He pressed the remote for the camera and captured the moment. Then he picked up a large knife and plunged it into the man's stomach several times, taking plenty of photos of the victim's tortured screams. He plunged the knife into the man's heart to finish the task and then collected his blood in the same bottle that held the woman's.

He unchained the body and drug it to the walk-in cooler. He'd leave it there until he chose the perfect dumping spot. Then he poured bleach onto the floor and mopped up the mess.

Satisfied, he went upstairs to his studio and got to work on his latest masterpiece, using the photos to guide him. He filled the canvas with anger, denial, grief, pain, agony, and the acceptance of inevitable death before going to Larissa Ray's funeral. There would definitely be grief there. It was the perfect muse.

CHAPTER 13

WE WERE APPLAUDED when we got back to the station. Eric gestured to me, though, and told them, "Hey, this is all hers. She's the one who got the intel. I was just along for the ride."

I held up my empty coffee cup in a toast. "To good informants and quick search warrants."

They all cheered, "Here-here."

"We'll all have to get a real drink after work to celebrate," Eric jovially suggested, and it sounded good to everyone.

"Now, back to the Slasher case," Liam mumbled. "We didn't come up with anything new, so we're still at a stalemate until he kills again or fucks up. We still don't have any forensic evidence or suspects."

I tapped my desk in thought. "Since we don't know how long he's been refrigerating bodies, I wonder why he chose now to drop them in our laps." I looked at the blotter on my desk and doodled to help me concentrate. "Perhaps it has to do with the Fourth of July holiday weekend coming up," I theorized.

"But why?" Marisol questioned, and I couldn't answer…yet.

I shook my head out of frustration. "I don't know, but we have only a week to figure it out." I looked at my watch. It was already 5:45. "I'll have to have that drink when we finish this case," I announced and gathered my things up. "I'm going to go home and go over all this tonight."

"Me too. No rest for the weary when there's a crazed killer on the loose," Liam stated and grabbed his things as well.

"So, we'll all work tonight and compare notes in the morning then," Eric agreed.

We filed out to the parking lot, and I knew we were wondering the same thing. *What fresh hell will greet us tomorrow?*

After a light dinner, I spread my notes out on the dining room table along with some criminal investigation books. Duke wanted to play, so I engaged him in a game of fetch with his tennis ball while I worked. I was relieved that he was adjusting to his new home.

I wrote down anything I knew that had to be a given. For instance, the killer had to have a quiet secluded place to torture his victims, or someone would have reported the disturbances. Gunshots in the city were so common that they were often ignored, but not the sick shit this man was inflicting on his victims. I printed off a map of St. Louis and the surrounding areas and circled anywhere considered rural. I highlighted Eureka, Wildwood, Ellisville, and Town & Country to start. He also had to have enough room in his home or on his property for a large walk-in cooler. Unfortunately, Eric hadn't found records of any recent cooler purchases in the St. Louis area, so I jotted down a note to check in Illinois. Hell, for all we knew, he resided in Illinois.

I considered how he was transporting the bodies to the dump sites. He'd need trunk space or a large vehicle. Possibly, he had tinted windows on his vehicle. Without eyewitnesses, it was difficult to know. We couldn't even set up roadblocks since we didn't know where he was coming from. He was, so far, untraceable.

I thought about how he was kidnapping his victims, especially the men. How was he luring them or taking them by force? Chris's reports didn't say anything about taser burns, so he wasn't using that. Their toxicology screens came back clean, so he wasn't drugging them either.

Duke whimpered at my side, so I reached over and petted him between the ears.

"I know, buddy. It's getting late, and we should think about going to bed. Go potty for me," I told him and opened the back door.

While he was outside, I went online and looked up extra-large dog doors on Petco's website. They had some in stock, so I purchased one to pick up tomorrow. Of course, I needed someone to help me install it, and since Dave had left already, I thought about asking Eric to help. I heard Duke scratch on the door, so I let him back inside.

"Momma's shopping for you," I cooed to him just as my cell phone rang.

I expected it to be SLCPD calling with a new case or an update to the current one, so I was surprised to see Justin's name on the screen. With a sigh, I took the call this time.

"Yes, Justin?"

"Hi. I wanted to check up on you. I know about the case you're working on and how tough it is. You just live for danger, don't you?" His voice had a hint of teasing in it, but I knew he was serious.

"You know me. Besides, I'm not undercover, so it's not so bad," I replied.

I felt the tension radiating through the phone, and it gnawed at my stomach. Why was it perfectly fine for men to work in my field, but not women? They were in just as much danger as we were.

"I suppose," he finally mumbled. "Anyway, I called to see if I can take you out to dinner."

I glanced at the back door as a plan formed. "I've got a better idea. I need a dog door installed, so if you want to come over tomorrow night to help me with that, I'll *fix* you dinner."

"A dog door? You finally got a dog, or are you planning on getting one?" he wondered.

"I got one. I took my neighbor's dog because he was deployed again." I reached over and scratched Duke's head some more, which came well above my knee when we were both sitting.

"Hmm…what will you make for me?"

I giggled softly, "I'll make you a T-bone steak. I'll even fix it medium-well for you; although, I still don't understand how people can eat undercooked meat."

Laughing, he asked, "What time do you want me there?"

I looked down at my notes and told him, "Come over at 6:00. That way I'll have time to pick up the dog door after work."

"All right, I'll be there at 6:00, and I'll bring the wine," he stated. "Bye." He hung up before I could object to the alcohol. He knew wine loosened me up, and I figured it was his ploy.

I looked down at Duke. "It looks like we'll be having company tomorrow night, but don't get attached to him. I'm not taking that road again."

I pushed my notes aside and headed to my bedroom with Duke in tow. I checked the alarm clock and turned out the lamplight while he climbed into the bed next to me. I fell asleep with my arm over him. I felt so much safer with him there, and that was more important to me now than ever before. Not only did I have the elusive psycho serial killer we were chasing, but I was probably on the hit list for the Bloods since I arrested Carlos and two of his bangers.

I glanced over my shoulder at the nightstand where my gun and badge rested, focusing my eyes on the badge.

"You sure come with strings attached," I mused aloud.

CHAPTER 14

AFTER ADDING A few more brush strokes to the canvas, he went down to the cellar to give his new guest a sip of water. He couldn't have her dying of dehydration; it would spoil his fun. He smiled to himself as he relived the moment they'd met last night. He had found her waiting in the parking lot at the local truck stop. She was what they called a "lot lizard." She was a hooker looking to give her next ride. He had pretended to be a customer and told her he lived nearby. Then after she had climbed into his vehicle, the chloroform-soaked rag had rendered her unconscious.

"Good morning, dear," he said in a sickening-sweet tone. "How did you sleep?"

The woman's eyes were stained black from her eye makeup smearing in her tears, so she reminded him of a raccoon. "Did I sleep?" she snarled. "Who the fuck are you?"

He narrowed his eyes to mere slits. "You can call me John. Get it?"

She closed her eyes to blacken out his scornful face, but the sound of his approaching footsteps made her open them back up.

"Okay, I guess you're not in a joking mood," he stated. "But I do suppose you're thirsty, so I brought you a drink." He held the water up to her mouth, and she sniffed it, causing him to laugh. "Do you think I poisoned it? And if I did, would that be worse than this?" He gestured to the chains holding her against the wall.

"No, I guess not," she spat and accepted the water. When he pulled the bottle away, she pleaded, "Please let me go. I've not done anything to you. Why are you doing this?"

He found joy and amusement in her tears, so he took a photo. Then he answered her question. "I'm doing this simply because I can." He went back to snapping pictures.

Her expression hardened, but he could still see the fear in her eyes. "Why are you taking photos of me?" she demanded in a threatening tone.

He cocked his head and set his mouth in a hard line. "It's for my collage," he answered with authority in his voice. "However, you're not cooperating, so I need to correct that."

He approached her with a knife he had hidden in his pocket, and she screamed for help. Instead of covering her mouth with the duct tape, he surprised her by matching her volume with his own blood-curdling cries. She stopped her fit immediately.

"There's no use, so you might as well save your breath," he advised her. "You know, if I cut you right here"—he put the tip of his knife to her carotid—"you'd bleed out within minutes, but I'm not going to do that."

"Fuck you!" she spat at him and struggled against the chains until her skin was bloody and raw.

"If you recall, you tried to last night, and it didn't work then either. You're not my type," he remarked. "But I suppose you do have *something* I want."

"What do I have that you want?" she demanded.

"Blood and pain," he sneered and sliced through her pants and into her thigh muscle.

He snapped several photos of her despair. It was like porn for him.

"I have to go for now, but I'll be back later to pick up where we left off," he threatened.

She yelled a string of obscenities as he climbed up the stairs, and it made him laugh. She definitely had spirit.

CHAPTER 15

BEFORE I WENT to work on Thursday, I put the T-bone steaks in a pan of sauces and spices to marinate. I had to laugh at Duke because he watched attentively and licked his chops.

"Don't worry, buddy. I left a thick steak out just for you," I promised him.

I fed him while he did his morning business, and then I kissed him goodbye and left for work.

Traffic was better than yesterday, so I arrived on time, and so did the others. Eric had the coffees for everyone this time.

"I'll bring them in tomorrow, just write down your preferences for me," I volunteered.

In unison, they called out, "Black," and I was relieved. It was difficult to remember all the half-this, one-pump-that combinations offered at Starbucks.

"Did anybody think of anything new last night?" Eric probed.

I pulled out my marked maps and told them my thoughts. Funnily, Marisol had done the same thing.

"Well, we could get in touch with the police departments in those areas and see if they'll help us search," Liam offered. "Maybe dogs can sniff around the woods."

I also interjected an idea. "We can contact the St. Louis County Assessor's Office and ask the Real Property Division about any homes with outbuildings large enough to hold a walk-in cooler or special permits to build attached ones onto the home."

"Excellent idea," the lieutenant called out from behind me. "I'm glad to see you are all finding ways to track this perp. Hopefully, we'll have him in custody soon."

I tucked my dark hair behind my ear while I chewed on his words. "What if it's not a man? What if it's a strong woman? That might explain the lack of sexual assault, and also how the perp is abducting men. She might not even have to be big or strong if she uses something to overpower them."

Eric cocked his head at me, and I could see his wheels turning. "But the tox screens came back clean, and there aren't any wounds to suggest a taser was used, so how else could she subdue them?"

"Chloroform would work," I suggested, "and you have to be specifically looking for it."

Marisol picked up her desk phone and began dialing. "I'm calling Chris to have him check the male victim if the body is still here."

We all waited quietly for her to finish the call. She didn't look pleased. "Damn. Tucker Brown has already been released to the funeral home."

I tried to stay positive and told them, "Well, now he knows to check for it. He should also check for scopolamine next time." I jotted a note down on my blotter so I wouldn't forget to ask. *Next time?* I knew there would be one.

We spent the day searching through the records we retrieved from the St Louis County Assessor's Office, and there were a lot of them. Several residents in the rural areas we were primarily focused on had outbuildings or special permits for attached structures, which came as a surprise to me. It didn't mean they were for walk-in coolers, though, so the police were going to have to knock on doors. *We* were going to have to knock on doors as well, but not today. It was quitting time.

I went straight to Petco and picked up my dog door and then headed home. Justin was already parked along the curb even though I was a few minutes early.

"Here, let me get that for you," he offered and took hold of the large box.

"Thank you," I mumbled and got the door for us. It was hard not to laugh when Duke almost knocked him over.

"Damn, that's a big dog!" he yelped. "What kind is he?"

I told Duke to sit, which he did, and answered, "He's a Belgian Malinois and a very good boy."

Justin eyed my pet suspiciously. "I'll take your word for it. I don't care much for big dogs." He gestured toward my kitchen. "Do you have the tools I need? If not, I brought a set."

I opened my hall closet and drug out my single woman's toolkit and drill. "This should work."

"Really?" he joked when he accepted the lightweight box. "This is your go-to toolkit?"

I put my hands on my hips and stuck my chin out. "I've never needed anything more."

He laughed at me and walked into the kitchen while shaking his head. He set the box down, examined the door, and then walked back toward the living room.

"I need to get a reciprocating saw out of my car," he announced.

While he did that, I started supper. I was going to fix a tossed salad, baked potatoes, and corn on the cob as our side dishes. I added another coat of marinade to the steaks and put them in the oven to broil, making sure to set the timer, so I would get his out before it turned well-done.

He came back in, and Duke jumped up from the kitchen floor to check things out. I assumed he recognized Justin's cologne since he didn't bark or growl.

"Your butler let me in," Justin teased.

I winked at him. "You're lucky. He normally asks for a cover charge." I noticed the saw in his right hand and a bottle of Chardonnay in his left. *Shit. I thought he forgot about it.*

He took the door off its hinges, carried it out to the backyard, and started working on it until I called him in for dinner. I set the third steak aside to cool off for Duke, and Justin noticed.

"Are you eating two steaks? I don't think I'll have room for seconds," Justin chuckled and patted his stomach.

I shot him a dirty look. "No, silly. That one is for Duke."

He looked at the dog, who was curled up by my chair, and shook his head. "Spoiled already. Why am I not surprised?"

I put the food on the table, ignoring his assessment, and then cut Duke's steak up so it would cool faster. Justin reached into the cupboard around me for wine glasses.

"No-no-no, Mr. Sinclair," I chastised him. "There will be no alcohol consumption until you're done with the dog door. I'm not responsible for missing fingers around here."

"Oh yeah? What about missing limbs because of that two-hundred-pound furball?" he joked.

I shrugged. "If he has to protect me from bad guys, so be it."

"Uh-huh. Tell me about your case. How's it going?" he inquired, and I saw the concern etched on his face.

Here we go again. "Well, you probably already know as much as we do. We don't have any hint of a suspect yet, and we don't have any trace."

He rubbed his jaw, looking frustrated. "That just makes my job harder, you know? You're going to have to give me something to work with when this goes to trial."

I dipped my head and glared at him. "But no pressure, right? I'm sure by the time this goes to trial, we'll have everything we need."

He picked up his mess and went back to work on the door while I cleaned up the kitchen and put the leftover side dishes away.

"Here you go, buddy," I called out to Duke and flopped the meat on top of his dog food. He ate it all in a matter of a few bites. "You *could* take off a limb, couldn't you?"

Twenty minutes later, Justin got the door back up on its hinges, complete with a monstrous-size doggie door, and poured two glasses of wine. I took one, against my better judgment, and sat on the sofa with him. I turned on the TV as a distraction technique, and there was a documentary on about Jack the Ripper.

"Liam is calling our investigation the 'Slasher case' now. Isn't that something?" I blurted out.

He sighed heavily and scrunched his face. "The problem with naming cases like that is the media will get ahold of it, and then the killer will hear it and feel immortalized. It gives him too much power."

I couldn't deny the truth in his words. The killer would get his jollies off knowing he would become a legend—the infamous St. Louis Slasher.

I turned to him to respond, but he didn't give me a chance. His mouth smashed against mine while a groping hand roamed up my side to my breast. I pushed against him, but I didn't do it hard enough. I was conflicted. We had six months together, and I was so stressed out by the case. I gave in to his tempting touch and lost myself in the moment. *Just tonight. I'll relent, but only for tonight.*

CHAPTER 16

HE DRAGGED THE man's corpse out of the cooler and loaded it into his vehicle. Then he drove around until he found the perfect spot. He was careful to obey all traffic rules and regulations, so he wasn't pulled over.

When he turned into the hospital parking lot, he found a dark corner to park in. Then he pulled his hat down over his eyes and retrieved a wheelchair from the side entrance. His idea tickled him, and it was all he could do to keep from laughing aloud. He propped the victim up in the seat and pushed him to the parking garage, where he left him in a handicap slip. It was a hot and humid night; therefore, he would thaw out perfectly by morning. He'd probably even reek of decomposition. *Oh well. Occupational hazard for them I suppose.*

He used the inspiration to go back to his studio. His latest portrait was almost complete. While he splashed the paint onto the canvas, the sound of rattling chains from the basement encouraged him. He smiled broadly as he heard shouts for an encore. So, when he was satisfied with his creation, he set the painting off to the side to dry and began another. This one would have a lot of red. He loved the color of blood. He worked on it for thirty minutes before checking up on his most recent guest.

"And how are you enjoying your stay with us?" he asked with a maniacal laugh. "Is the food to your liking?"

He looked down at the floor and the empty ham bone he'd tossed there the night before. He'd left some meat on it that time—just enough for the rats. The critters were hiding now, watching and waiting for the taste of blood. He wouldn't dream of disappointing them.

He approached the hooker, who then bellowed, "Just kill me if that's what you intend to do anyway. Just get it over with."

He made a long line of red across her collarbone, soaking up every note of her ear-piercing screams. He didn't need to take photos this time. The image was burned into the deep recesses of his twisted mind—until it ended up on his canvas in a museum exhibit. He looked at his watch and decided to go to bed. He felt restless, but he had an early morning appointment regarding his artwork.

"Sweet dreams," he called out to the broken woman and trotted up the stairs. He could already hear the rats squeaking.

CHAPTER 17

I ALMOST FORGOT to get the coffees Friday morning because I was engrossed in my thoughts about Justin. Making love again was likely a big mistake, but I couldn't worry about that now. *What's done is done.* I had to focus on the case.

We convened in the conference room with the lieutenant and went over everything we had. Every speculation was carefully examined.

"Eric, you checked NCIC already for similar murders, right?" I asked.

He nodded and addressed the group. "Yes, I checked, and there aren't any homicides that match our guy. While torture isn't unique, his particular methods are."

I rubbed the back of my neck. I needed to get a professional massage. "How is he not leaving any trace? Gloves are a given, but there aren't any hairs or anything. I guess he could be bald," I conjectured.

"He might also shave his body," Marisol added. "I wonder if he's impotent, and that's why he's not raping them."

We all agreed that was possible, and we considered the possibility, again, that it might be a woman we were after.

"But like you said after the first victim was found, it's unlikely a woman would cut another woman's face up," Liam reminded me.

"You're right. I did say that." I put my head in my hands and moaned. "I'm getting so turned around in this case. It's eating me up."

The lieutenant stood up and suggested we proceed with knocking on doors along with the local law enforcement in the areas we were concentrating on. We had our list of dwellings with special licenses, so there was no time like the present to tackle it.

"Ask the departments in person, though, and let them copy the list and section it off, so you don't duplicate searches. Keep the lines of communication open with them," he commanded.

"Will do, Boss," Liam responded on our behalf. "Let's divide the territory up."

We decided that Marisol and I would go to Wildwood, while he and Eric headed to Ellisville, and we parted ways.

Marisol drove the unmarked car, and on the way, we compared our careers on the force, and then she asked about my marital status.

"I noticed you're not wearing a wedding ring. Is that because you're single, or are you protecting your family like I am?" She held up her left arm and wiggled her vacant finger.

"I'm still single," I sighed. "I suppose you could say that I'm married to the job." I turned to face her. "How does your husband cope with you being on the force?"

Her lips turned up in a half-smile. "I didn't give him a choice. It was a meet-cute. I met him when I arrested him for brawling in a bar. When I broke it up, he told me with a slur that they were fighting over me, which of course was silly since I wasn't there until the 911 call came in." She laughed to herself. "Anyway, after he made bail, he asked me for my number, and I denied him, so he kept sending flowers to the station until it looked like my desk was entered in the Rose Parade. Every bouquet had a card with a cute message and his number."

I laughed from the mental image her story inspired. "And you called him," I finished for her.

She nodded with another giggle. "That was four years ago, and we've been together since."

"Did he ever ask you to give it up?" I inquired.

She shook her head and turned into the Wildwood Police Station parking lot. "No, he knows how dedicated I am to my career."

I sighed, "That's nice. I haven't found that yet. I was dating ADA Sinclair, but he hated my undercover work in the Drug Unit, so we fell by the wayside."

"Wow. I'm sorry to hear that," she replied.

I climbed out of the car with a shrug. "It doesn't matter. I've got the perfect man in my life now—my dog."

We laughed and entered the station, flashing our badges at the receptionist. "May we have a word with the chief of police, please?" Marisol asked.

We had to wait eight minutes before Chief Meyer fetched us and led us back to his office. "What can I do for you?" he inquired.

We told him about the murders and our theories that led us to his doorstep, and he listened intently while making notes.

"I've seen the killings on the news, of course, but I never considered it to be someone from our community. I can't rule it out, though. These are crazy times with the election coming up this year," he commented.

"Well, we don't have reason to believe the murders have anything to do with that, and they aren't racially or economically motivated either. He's not showing any discrimination in choosing his victims," I said.

He clasped his hands together behind his head and leaned back in his chair. "So, I can give you a handful of officers to help you knock on doors, but without warrants, there's not a lot you can do. The residents have to be willing to show you the outbuildings or home amenities."

We both nodded. "We understand, but maybe we'll find probable cause somewhere that will get us the warrants we need," I suggested.

He sighed, "Fair enough. Give me a few minutes to round up some patrol officers. You can just wait here."

When he left the office, our phones rang. It was SLCPD summoning us back to Headquarters. There was another body found.

CHAPTER 18

HE WAITED IMPATIENTLY for the museum curator to come out of her office while clutching a portfolio and his most recently completed painting. It wasn't his first time in the museum. She had denied his work before, but he didn't think she would this time. If she did, though, he'd teach her a lesson she'd never forget.

"Thank you for waiting, Mr. Peirick," Tiffany Clark greeted him when she decided to grace him with her presence. "Joan told me you have something different for me to look at today." Her snooty tone told him that she expected to be disappointed again, and it irked his nerves.

"Yes, I do. I think you'll be quite pleased with what I have for you," he told her straightforward.

"All right, Mr. Peirick. Show me your work," she commented and made it sound like a chore.

He uncovered his canvas and turned it around for her to see. She tapped one perfectly manicured fingernail on her mahogany desk while she studied the piece. Her mouth bunched up to one side, and he couldn't gage her thoughts. She motioned for him to hand it over to her, and then she put on her reading glasses as she studied it up close.

"Your work is definitely better this time around. I can feel your thoughts when I look at it. It inspires emotion. It has depth," she complimented him but didn't smile.

In one quick gesture, he handed over his portfolio. "Here are some more examples of my new style."

She flipped through the book in a way that suggested he was wasting her time, and he felt his anger intensify. *This bitch has no idea what I can do to her.*

She cleared her throat and announced, "These are better as well, but not as much as this one"—she held the canvas up—"but it still lacks something. You're showing emotion, which is great, but it's still wavering"—she tapped the canvas, causing him to cringe—"Here, you have strong, confident strokes, but over here, they are hesitant and feeble."

He strained his eyes at the canvas to see what she was talking about, but all he could see was her slow, painful death.

She handed back the portfolio and canvas. "Tunnel your strength and try again. We have an art show coming up over the Fourth of July holiday where we'll be featuring new artists, and I think you could make it into the show. I just need to see a little more effort." Her clipped tone said they were done for now, but he knew they would see each other again very soon. *This is far from over, bitch!*

He put the canvas and his portfolio in his car and drove around town to cool off before going to his other job. Painting was his passion, but it didn't pay the bills just yet. It would soon, though. It had to.

CHAPTER 19

WE HURRIED BACK to the station and caught up with Eric and Liam in the parking lot. Instead of waiting on the elevator, we all rushed up the stairs to Homicide to find out the details.

Captain Russell Roman had just returned from vacation and took the reins back from the lieutenant. He summoned us into the conference room.

"I've been in Florida for the past two weeks, but I'm ready to get caught up," he stated.

"Didn't you say you had three weeks off?" Liam wondered.

"I did, but I couldn't stay away with this killer on the loose. The job will have to win out over my free time for now," he answered. "Although, I'm sure the lieutenant was doing a fine job in my absence."

Liam filled him in on everything we had on the killings, which certainly wasn't much.

"So, I called you back in because there has been another body found with the same MO. Andrew Adams, whose blood was discovered in the Fox Theater parking lot, was left in the parking garage at Barnes-Jewish hospital sometime last night. He was sitting up in a wheelchair, so the perp had to enter the hospital to get one. I have the crime lab looking at video surveillance footage of every entrance right now. Chris is waiting for you all to join him in the morgue for the autopsy. He wants to be thorough, so please go watch," the captain advised us.

We hustled back down the stairs to the frigid morgue and observed the autopsy. Chris narrated his findings to us, paying particular attention to anything that was different with this victim.

"His right knee was shattered and caused a large bone fragment to tear through the flesh, but he lacks the burn marks on his soles. I see signs of starvation again, and he has multiple stab wounds. It looks like his heart was stabbed too, likely causing his final demise."

I closed my eyes, cringing on the inside. I couldn't imagine anybody being so sick and twisted to do this to another human. Then I remembered the notes I'd jotted on my blotter.

"Chris, please swab his mouth and lungs for evidence of chloroform, and please check for scopolamine as well," I told him. "We have to find out how he is subduing his victims."

He collected the swabs and bagged them for the lab. I immediately took them into the crime lab for analysis and requested a rush on all evidence collected.

Jackie, the lead technician, informed me, "We don't have prints or foreign hairs with this one either." When the mass spectrometer was finished, it printed off the results, and I watched her face as she read the report. "There is trace evidence of chloroform from around the mouth but no evidence of scopolamine or other date rape drugs," she announced and handed me the report to put in the case file.

"Thank you. This helps us," I acknowledged and went back to the morgue to tell the others.

"Good call," Chris congratulated me. "I wish I could take the credit for that finding, but it's yours, Sasha."

"Now, is he buying the chloroform somewhere or making it himself?" I wondered aloud. "I know you can buy it for agricultural purposes, but you can also make it using household bleach, acetone, and ice."

Eric narrowed his eyes at me with a half-smile. "You sure know a lot about the subject."

I shrugged. "I read. In any case, he'd have to be extremely careful in producing it and using it because too high a concentration is lethal. So, he must've done his research to use just enough to knock out his victims without killing them, and he must have a well-ventilated work area to produce it."

"Like you said, he could be buying it online for livestock use," Marisol added, and I nodded in affirmation.

"That would be impossible to trace since stores don't carry the stuff," Liam grumbled.

I pointed a finger in the air and replied, "However, if we find a suspect and search his computer, then…"

Chris interrupted, "Official cause of death for this young man is sudden cardiac arrest. Of course, with stab wounds this deep, he would have bled out if his heart hadn't given out first."

While he stitched the body back up, we went upstairs, taking the elevator this time.

"Why did he change up his behavior?" I asked them, referring to the lack of burns and the shattered knee.

Eric replied, "It's hard to say. Maybe it's because it's a male victim. The man found at SLU had broken bones too."

"But he was also burned, and why just break bones in the men?" I pressed.

"Perhaps because it's easier to control them, or possibly to inflict more pain," Liam suggested.

I got to thinking about the lack of rape. "It could point to impotence. Maybe he's punishing them for being more of a man than he is," I suggested, and they agreed that it was possible.

I grabbed a baked good from the vending machine to eat at my desk while I combed over my notes. I drew circles on a piece of paper with the names of the victims split up one to a circle. I listed what had happened to each victim in their final hours within the circle and then marked the common denominators. I also listed their personal information, and there still wasn't anything overlapping. He had to be choosing them at random.

My desk phone rang and made me jump in my chair. "Detective Delossa," I answered. There was only the sound of heavy breathing on the other end, so I repeated myself.

"I read about you in the paper, detective. How are you enjoying your promotion?" The voice on the other end was deep and muffled.

"I'm enjoying it just fine. Can I help you with something?" I asked while still working on my notes.

"I also read about the arrest you made recently. I bet there are a lot of pissed off gang members out looking for you," the man continued. "What I want to know, however, is if you're so smart, why can't you find me?" He laughed and then hung up before I could utter another word.

I put the phone back in the cradle and stared at it while my body trembled. *Clearly, our killer is not only smart, he is also into mind games.*

Marisol sat down in her chair and stared at me. "What's wrong? You look like you just saw a ghost," she observed.

"He called me," I stated without looking at her. "The killer just called me." I looked up, and her eyes were bulging just like mine were.

Eric overheard me and rushed to my desk and asked, "What did he say to you?"

I repeated what the killer had told me just as Liam rounded the corner. "What happened?" he wondered, and I explained once more.

"Shit! He's taunting us. He is dropping bodies on our doorstep like a proud cat with mice, and he wants to brag about it," Liam shouted.

I stood up and paced the room. "Reaching out is just part of his narcissism, and I'm sure he'll do it again."

"But why you? Why did he contact you directly?" Eric inquired, and the question was valid and something I was already considering.

I rubbed my neck. "He said he read that article on my promotion in the paper, and he also read about us arresting Garcia. I suppose, though, he's trying to test the new girl." I laughed nervously. "I have to admit that it worked."

"It worked on us all," Eric mumbled. "What affects you affects the whole team."

Jackie approached us with a photo in hand. "I've finished with the surveillance footage, and this is the only person fetching a wheelchair. It's timestamped 10:28 last night"—she flipped the photo around for us—"With his hat pulled down, though, we can't see his face in any of the footage."

"He was deliberately avoiding the cameras, and no one walked past him either. It was from a more secluded entrance, wasn't it?" I questioned.

She nodded. "Yes, it's from the side entrance that's around the corner from the ER."

Liam took the photo from her and thanked her for bringing it up to us. "He looks to be around six feet tall, but he could be hunching over. At least we know he's white with brown hair and has an average build. That's a start."

Marisol rolled her eyes. "It's still not much, but I suppose it's more than we had, so we should be glad about that."

I was only half-listening because my mind had drifted elsewhere. *Is he watching me too?*

I drove straight home and kept my cop eye out for any vehicles that might be following me. I parked in my garage as opposed to the driveway like I normally did. Even if he wasn't watching me, the Bloods might be. My address and phone number were unlisted, but still, criminals had a way.

Duke barked with a low growl at the door that led from the garage into my kitchen. "It's okay, buddy. It's just me," I called out, and he began whimpering. I unlocked the door and punched in my alarm code on the keypad. "There's my good boy," I said softly and petted him.

He followed me through the house as I put my purse and badge on the nightstand in the bedroom. I almost set my Glock down, too, but then I thought better of it. I kept it tucked in its holster on my hip and kicked off my standard issue cop boots. I changed out of my required blue shirt and slacks and threw them in the washer before feeding Duke and working on my own dinner.

I looked at him while I ate my spaghetti. He was sitting protectively next to my chair, so I tossed him a meatball.

"I just don't know about this case," I mumbled. "I wish you were a police dog at times like this. Maybe you could see something we aren't."

Justin called while I was loading the dishwasher. He said he hoped we could get together again, and I moaned to myself.

"I don't know, Justin," I sighed. "Nothing has changed between us. You—"

He interrupted, "Yes it has. I had a problem with you being undercover, not with you being a cop. You aren't going to be undercover anymore, so everything has changed."

I flopped on the sofa with a grunt. "I don't know. Last night was kind of nice, but I'm too wrapped up in work right now to consider anything else. After this case is over, then maybe…"

"But then there will be another case, so is that going to be your excuse then too?" he asked, and I heard the frustration in his voice.

"Yes, there will always be another case. What that means for you and me, well, I don't know," I professed. "I can't make any promises."

There was an awkward silence before he told me he had to go and hung up. I blew out a rush of air and rubbed my eyes.

"Duke, I'm so glad you're not a complicated man," I moaned and stroked his back.

He looked up at me with love in his eyes before flopping down, so his belly was exposed. I gave him a good scratching and then took a relaxing bath before bed. I'd brought my files home, but I couldn't deal with any more horror today.

CHAPTER 20

HE PACED THE floorboards of his studio. It was the smaller of the two he had, but he liked it all the same. He just couldn't concentrate on his work because the curator had dismissed his talents…again. He'd teach her a lesson—that was a given. First, though, he had to make room or, at the very least, install more chains. With a smile, he went to his garage and gathered supplies. Then he went to the basement to check on his guest.

"Are you thirsty?" he asked her with mock politeness.

"Yes." Her voice was so scratchy he could hardly understand her, and she was too weak to nod.

"Here, drink this. It will make you less hungry." He held a straw to her mouth that was stuck inside a meal replacement shake, and she quickly sucked it all down until he heard the slurping of air. He pulled it away saying, "See? I'm not that cruel."

"Then please just let me go," she wept for the hundredth time. "I have a child, and he needs me."

He cocked his head at her. "I could let you go if I wanted to, but I've had a rough day today, so I need the company. Misery loves company, right? Do you know what my father did to me when he had a rough day?"

Tears trickled down her dark, hollow cheeks. "Was he mean to you?"

He laughed in response and told her, "Mean? He was a monster. He'd beat me with his belt until I had whelps all over my body. Then"—he held up his palm for her—"he'd place my hand on the hot stove just for the hell of it."

"I'm sorry," she sobbed.

He stepped closer, assessing her current pitiful condition. "That's what my mother used to say too. She'd tell me how sorry she was, but she never did anything to stop him." He grabbed her jaw and made her stare into his eyes. "Don't worry, my pet. I'm not going to slap you around like he did me, and I won't put your hand to the stove either. However, I can't let you go. No one was around to witness my pain, but the whole world is going to see yours." He reached out with the knife and sliced her across the abdomen. Over her screams, he told her, "If I'd cut any deeper, your guts would be hanging out. You're welcome." He held the camera up. *Click. Click.*

With a low chuckle, he walked to the opposite wall and began pounding a new set of chains into the concrete. The noise was deafening and almost drowned her screams out. He yanked on the cuffs to ensure their strength and then turned back to his victim.

"You're going to have company soon, so do be sure to hang on. You don't want to miss it." He laughed again and headed back up the stairs to paint while he had the inspiration.

CHAPTER 21

I STILL WOKE up at 6:00 on Saturday even though I had the day off work. We were all on call over the weekend, however, and I'd be working on my notes too. I'm sure the rest of the team would be doing the same.

Before it warmed up more, I put on a T-shirt and shorts and took Duke for an early morning jog around the neighborhood. Actually, he took *me* for a jog since the massive dog pulled on the leash in his excitement to be out running. I knew Dave used to go running with him, but he didn't keep him on the leash. I was just afraid Duke would take off to go look for his former daddy. After a quarter-mile, however, I gave up and unclasped him. He surprised me when he stayed faithfully by my side.

We were on the last stretch toward home when a car heading toward us slowed down. We were at least a half-mile from the house yet, and of course, I didn't have my gun. I wouldn't have cared, but the men inside the car looked like they were up to no good. The car came to a stop, and the passengers began making lude catcalls while the driver opened his door. Before he could climb out, though, Duke charged the car and jumped on the hood to stare him down with a ferocious growl. The driver closed the door and honked the car horn, but Duke held his stance.

"Damn bitch, call off your dog!" one of the passengers yelled out the window.

With a smile, I approached the car on the driver's side. "It's awfully early for you boys to be stinking up the neighborhood, don't you think?"

The driver looked down, and I prepared myself in case he drew a gun. "Get your dog, lady, and we'll be on our way," he grumbled.

"Be sure that you are," I told him, and then I whistled for Duke to follow me.

I made sure they were no longer around before I went home. I certainly didn't need the thugs to know where I reside. After a quick shower, I fixed sausage and eggs for breakfast and fed half to Duke.

"Who's Momma's tough and protective boy?" I cooed while scratching his head. "You did a great job, but I think I'll carry my Glock next time too." I laughed to myself. *Were you packing heat? No, I was packing fur.*

After I cleaned up the breakfast mess, I kept going and cleaned the whole house. Soon, it was early afternoon, and I was left with nothing else to do, so I tackled the files on my coffee table while I had the movie *Copycat* on in the background for inspiration.

"Is that what you're after too, dickhead? Are you seeking fame in the media?" I questioned aloud.

I went over everything, trying to find a common denominator, but I came up empty. Not even the hair or eye color of the victims matched, so he clearly didn't have a type he was looking for, which struck me as unusual. If he was committing these heinous murders strictly at random, he had to have a lot of rage bottled up, and I wondered why. Normally, the victims had common traits because they served as surrogates for the real target of the killer's rage, but this man seemed to hate everyone. I considered the possibility that he was a former soldier who had been at war and suffered from PTSD. It seemed likely that he'd witnessed torture firsthand. Given the lack of evidence at the crime scenes, I also considered the possibility that he currently was or had been a member of law enforcement. I jotted my thoughts down into lists of why each scenario made sense, and both options churned my stomach. I certainly didn't want to find out that a former hero had become a villain.

I was ready to take a break for a while when my cell phone rang. I grimaced before peeking at the display, expecting it to be the station, but it was my younger sister Denise. She was going into the criminal justice field too. She was studying law.

"Well, I've not heard from you in forever," I greeted her.

"You know the phone works both ways, right?" she teased. "Actually, I wanted to give you time to settle into your new position, but I see the ride has been bumpy."

I nodded on my end. "Yeah, it sure has been," I sighed. "How's school going?"

"It's fine, but I'm taking the summer off for a change," she informed me. "What can you tell me about this case you're on?"

I rolled my eyes. She was always inquisitive, which made her a strong student. "You know I can't discuss the particulars of an ongoing investigation," I groaned.

"I know, but I'm going to be a prosecutor someday," she reminded me.

"Well, when that day arrives, then we'll talk." I laughed because I could picture her pouting.

We discussed how our parents were doing, the guy she was involved with, and I told her about Duke. She asked me if I was still seeing Justin, and I almost disclosed that we'd had dinner together the other night, but I couldn't handle her reaction. She'd always told me I sold him short and should've tried harder to make it work. I, in turn, accused her of being prejudiced since he's the ADA. We chatted until her call waiting beeped.

"It's Marcus calling, so I need to go, but let's get together soon," she suggested, and I agreed.

I went into the kitchen to make a pitcher of iced tea. It was going to be in the upper nineties today, and I was already feeling it. I turned the thermostat down to seventy-three and sat back on the sofa with my tea and my dog to finish watching the movie.

"You know, Duke, if my life were like TV, I would've already caught the guy," I mumbled before curling up into a ball and falling asleep.

I was running through darkened alleys in the city in pursuit of a suspect. I didn't get a good look at his face, but I knew it was him. I was close and getting closer when I tripped over something and fell to the ground. I looked at the obstacle, and it was a dead body with multiple slash wounds. I felt for a pulse, but there wasn't even a faint heartbeat. I heard laughter in the distance, so I picked myself up and took off again.

As I neared the end of the alley, my view of cars zooming by was quickly blocked by the outline of several individuals, and I recognized the colors they wore—it was the Bloods gang. They drew their weapons, so I drew mine, but when I fired a warning shot, the gun jammed. I was as defenseless as a cat toy.

I turned back, but the dead woman had risen and was heading toward me.

"Why can't you catch him? I wouldn't have died if only you'd caught him," she moaned and had her arms out to strangle me.

Duke barked and made me jump upright on the couch. My heart was pounding in my ears, and I was glad he woke me up from the nightmare. I supposed, doing what I do, I could expect many more bad dreams to come—especially during this case. I took several deep breaths until my pulse returned to normal. Then I got up and got ready to go do my grocery shopping. I needed to take advantage of my time off while I still had it.

CHAPTER 22

HE SCROLLED THROUGH all the photos and chose the ones with the most suffering to be his muse. Then he painted his dark thoughts on the pure white canvas until it looked like something from a horror movie or a bad dream. He stepped back to examine his progress and felt like something was missing. It had plenty of fear, but it needed more pain. He grabbed the camera and went to the cellar.

The hooker yanked against her chains, cursing him all the while. "You can't keep me here forever, you piece of shit!" she spat. "Do you fucking hear me? I hope you burn in hell!"

He calmly approached her with the large knife, but something she said caught his attention and gave him an idea—a superbly morbid idea.

"Thank you," he told her and walked off toward the attached garage.

Moments later, he stood before her with a container of paint thinner, a large paint brush, a plastic funnel, and a pair of rubber gloves.

Her eyes bulged out of their sockets, and she demanded, "What is that? What are you doing?"

With a sadistic smile, he donned the gloves. "You have given me a wonderful idea," he growled while setting the tripod up. "And to answer your question, since I'm in a good mood, this is paint thinner."

"What for?" she shrieked. "What are you going to do to me?"

He smiled again and approached her while whispering, "I'm going to take ten years off your face with a chemical peel. You're welcome."

She thrashed against the cuffs so hard that her wrists broke. The snapping sound of bone and her screams accompanying it made him light up much like his father had done during one of his many beatings. He poured enough thinner onto the paint brush to saturate it before sweeping it across her face. Her screams bounced off the walls while her skin turned scalding-red and began to blister. He took several photos to capture the magnificent moment.

Her body went into convulsions, causing her head to bang relentlessly against the concrete wall while her eyes rolled back. He didn't want her to knock herself out or worse. That's not the ending he desired. He scrambled to grab the funnel, forced it into her mouth past her writhing tongue, and then poured in the lethal chemical. Foam came up her throat, spilling past her lips and making her look like a rabid animal. He took photos until her body ceased its twitching.

He eased her carcass out of the chains and tossed her into the walk-in cooler. Then he mopped up the floor and went upstairs to paint.

His strokes were strong and steady as he filled the canvas with suffering, pain, hatred, and death. The only thing the masterpiece was missing was remorse, and that was exactly how he wanted it.

CHAPTER 23

I WAS EATING breakfast on Sunday when my cell phone rang. This time it was SLCPD calling. The officer told me I needed to promptly arrive at the Trainwreck Saloon in Westport Plaza because another body had been found.

I threw on my blue shirt and slacks, strapped on my hardware, and rushed to the crime scene where I bumped into Marisol in the parking lot.

"Do you know any of the specifics yet?" I had to ask.

"No, I was just told a body was found," she replied.

I groaned, "Can't crime take the weekend off?"

We approached the crowd, blocked off by the ugly yellow tape, and she tossed over her shoulder, "That sure would be nice, wouldn't it?"

Liam and Eric were already there waiting for us. Liam motioned us over, and then he explained the owner discovered the unidentified female when he showed up to open the restaurant for the day.

"He said when he unlocked the patio doors, she was lying on the ground. He promised that he didn't touch a thing, and he kept the employees out of the area too," Liam informed us. "Eric and I looked at her, but we want your unbiased assessments, so go ahead and see her for yourself. Chris should be here soon, too."

I motioned to Marisol, and we brushed past the crime scene technicians who were already processing the scene. I gasped when I saw the woman's face.

"Oh my God! That's awful," I exclaimed with a gag.

The woman's red face was distorted with blisters and skin that was peeling away. The stench was horrific.

"It's also new," she added. "And look, her wrists are broken."

I looked back at the human remains. "But those gashes in her body aren't new, and Tucker Brown also had broken wrists." A thought occurred to me. "It could be they accidentally broke their wrists from struggling against their restraints." I asked a technician for gloves and put them on before lifting her wrist to examine it. "Her skin is raw. She definitely rubbed it against her cuffs." I looked at the inside of her arm. "I see old track wounds. She had been hooked on something once upon a time."

"Mind if I take a look?" Chris asked, startling me. I hadn't realized he'd joined us.

"No, of course not," I replied and got out of his way. He used a cotton swab around her mouth and smelled it. Then he opened her mouth and looked inside.

"What do you think it is?" I inquired.

His mouth was set in a tight line. "It smells like acetone, and it was poured down her throat as far as I can tell from this initial examination. I'll know more when I do the autopsy."

Marisol and I both gaped in horror. "Who could be this cruel? Are there no boundaries this sick bastard won't cross?" she exclaimed.

"Poor woman," I groaned.

Chris motioned for the morgue technicians to remove the body. "I'll get started right away. If he used chloroform on her, I doubt I'll find trace around her mouth. Perhaps I might find it in her lungs, but I can't guarantee it since she inhaled the toxic fumes from the acetone. I'll have her prints ran through IAFIS."

"Thank you," Marisol said on our behalf, and we followed the men out to the parking lot.

"I think we need to call the FBI in," Liam grumbled. "This is too much for just us." He pinched the bridge of his nose and squeezed his eyes shut. "I'll talk to the captain about it."

We climbed into our cars and drove back to SLCPD. During the drive, I couldn't help but think we were trying to catch the invisible man.

While Liam spoke to Captain Roman, the rest of us gathered in the bullpen and discussed our thoughts.

"Do you usually call in the FBI?" I asked them.

Eric cleared his throat and told me, "No, but then we don't usually have serial killers like this one. Normally, it's gang-related violence when we see multiple deaths"—he slammed his fist on his desk—"I don't think even those thugs are capable of such cruelty as this."

Liam came out of the captain's office and summoned us to follow him into the conference room. "The captain agrees that we need to rely on the FBI's help, so he's going to start making calls. Of course, in the meantime, we'll keep working the case from every angle, so what do we make of his change-up in MO with this victim?"

I doodled on my note pad while I thought about it. "Chris said the chemical used on her face and likely poured down her throat smelled like acetone. Besides nail polish remover, what else contains that?" I wondered aloud.

Liam wrote the word on the dry erase board and listed nail polish remover underneath it. Then, as we rattled items off, he added those too. We told him household cleaners, paint thinners, and automotive chemicals. There were several items that we found online and were able to exclude such as suntan lotion, paint, and sealants.

"We'll just have to wait on the lab report to see what the other compounds are to know exactly what was used," Eric stated.

As if on cue, Jackie knocked on the door. "I have some reports on your victim, and Dr. Edwards told me to bring them up right away." She flipped through the pages and told us, "Her prints were in IAFIS from when she was arrested for solicitation. She's Lara Reynolds, and her last known address was in East St. Louis. The chemicals found around her mouth are turpentine, mineral spirits, methyl ethyl ketone, and acetone. Those are the components of paint thinner. Dr. Reynolds will have more for you when he's finished with the autopsy."

Liam spoke on our behalf, "Thank you, Jackie." He accepted the reports and put them in the case's file box. Then he addressed us again, "House painters would have a use for paint thinner, so maybe we are looking for someone in contracting. Maybe he built his own outbuilding for a walk-in cooler too."

"There are a lot of construction companies around the St. Louis area, or he could even work independently," I stated.

"Either way, he could be using that to approach people. He could be asking them if they want work done," Marisol added.

"I don't think he's doing that because they aren't missing from their homes," Eric said, and I nodded in agreement with his assessment.

I thought about the recent victim. "If Lara Reynolds was still turning tricks, he could've approached her for that," I offered. "But what about the others? I recall that Tucker Brown was a mechanic and Andrew Adams worked for a butcher shop. Do they use paint thinner to remove paint from cars?" I wondered.

"No, they use paint stripper for that, and it's a different list of ingredients," Liam answered. "Good question, though."

Another knock on the doorframe made our heads snap up. It was Chris this time, and he walked in with his reports.

"She died of asphyxiation from the methylene chloride fumes, and my findings suggest that she had a seizure before her untimely death. Since her lungs were filled with the fumes, I wasn't able to find any trace of chloroform," he informed us.

"That's okay. We think that, given her profession, she went with him willingly," I stated.

"Okay, well, she had multiple stab wounds just like the others, and her wrists were broken too," he added. "She had a contusion on the back of her head, but she could have struck it when she had the seizure."

"Could he have hit her, causing the seizure?" I asked.

He sighed, "I didn't find tool markings to suggest blunt force trauma, so I don't think he did."

"Was she starved too?" Liam queried.

Chris clasped his hands together in front of himself and replied, "Yes, he had starved her too, but she had liquid in her bladder, so he did give her water, just not much by the looks of things. Lastly, I think she broke her own wrists against the cuffs in her attempt to escape."

I looked down at the table and felt ready to cry. I couldn't imagine being that afraid for your life, and I hoped I never would be. She'd given up all hope of being rescued and tortured herself to try to get away from the madman. No matter what, we had to stop him before he could do this to anyone else. *If he isn't already.*

The captain stepped up behind Chris and announced, "Three agents from the FBI are here to speak with you. I'll show them in."

CHAPTER 24

HE WOKE UP feeling restless, so he went back to his painting. Killing the tramp had given him a fresh outlook on his work, but the high would only last for so long, so he needed a fresh body. He could have held onto her for a while longer, but he wanted to toy with the police, especially the new detective. He pulled out the newspaper clipping about her promotion to the Homicide Unit and used her photo to sketch on a blank canvas. She was an attractive woman, and he would add the new art to his personal collection when it was finished. Or, he thought wickedly, perhaps he would send it to her as a gift.

He dipped the brush into the blood-mixed red paint and outlined her face and hair. He thought about switching to the black paint to match the color of her hair, but the crimson-red was so pretty, that he decided this piece would go into his *red* collection. However, he used a tray and mixed a dab of the black with the red to make it darker. It looked perfect. He used the same mixture to outline her facial features and then to fill in her lips. Then he switched to a wider brush and slashed across the canvas to fill in the background with the lighter mix. The irony of surrounding the detective's face with so much DNA was laughable. He'd collected the essence of every victim so far and blended it into the perfect hue.

"The color of death," he whispered to himself with a catty smile.

While the portrait dried, he went to the other house to check on his prisoner. "You're not looking well, my dear," he drawled when he saw her.

She looked up with lunacy in her eyes. "That's because you're killing me," she seethed through gritted teeth. "Get on with it or just let me go!"

He cocked his head to the side and smiled at her. "Are you afraid to die?"

"No," she growled.

He laid out a kit on the table near her, and her eyes bulged when she saw the instruments inside. Some were metal, thin-bladed, and razor-sharp, while others were an assortment of pliers.

"Are you afraid of *how*?" he taunted, and her reply choked off in her throat.

Her tears did the talking for her. She squeezed her eyes shut to either hide them or to make the vision of him go away like a nightmare. When she opened them again, he laughed.

"I'm still here. Don't worry, darling. I don't think I'm going to kill you today. Tomorrow looks better." He reached for a set of pliers and thrust them toward her face.

She pursed her lips tight, trying to keep him from her mouth, but he clamped hard onto her nose and twisted until there was a loud popping sound followed by her piercing screams. Her distorted face was the perfect picture. It was kind of like a Picasso painting. He took several snapshots and ran up the stairs to make use of the inspiration.

Vivid colors splashed onto the stark white canvas, filling it with wild energy. Each color represented a different emotion until it was a creative mess of anguish, fear, pain, and grief. It told a grim and foreboding story. It was someone's living nightmare, but not his. It was his *masterpiece.*

CHAPTER 25

THREE SERIOUS LOOKING agents entered the room and stood by the dry erase board after giving us and the board a once-over. The lone man introduced them.

"I am Agent Mark Pullum, and this is Agent Tina Amos and Agent Amelia Gould. We are here in an advisory capacity to assist you in the capture of your recent serial killer, who has been dubbed the 'St. Louis Slasher' according to the media."

I studied the brooding man, wondering if he ever smiled. Actually, I had to wonder if any of them ever smiled. Liam introduced each of us, and then we showed them our poker hand, pulling everything out of the evidence box.

"We still intend to knock on doors alongside the local police in those highlighted rural communities," Liam informed them.

"Good," Agent Pullum said. "I think that's wise. It might scare him enough to make him get sloppy."

I couldn't help but play the devil's advocate. "Or it might make him pick up the pace," I blurted.

Agent Gould spoke for the first time. "That's a possibility, but then it just makes it more likely he'll screw up and give something away."

"We'll be standing by, ready to secure any warrants you might need," Agent Amos added. "We have a few judges who are expeditious for us, and if you need backup, we'll be ready for that too."

When all was said and done, it looked like tomorrow was going to be the start of an extremely busy week for us.

I went home when we were finished talking and tried to salvage the rest of the day. I got caught up on my laundry and took Duke to a nice dog park in the area where I tossed the frisbee for him. There was a rain breeze kicking up, tousling my hair all around my face, but it felt good against the sun beating down on us through the gathering clouds.

We made it back inside the house just as the first drops began to fall. It didn't take long for the splatter to turn into a torrential thunderstorm, and I heard the warning sirens sound. I flipped on the news and saw that the county was under a tornado watch. I had emergency flashlights plugged in and charged, so if the power went out, we wouldn't be in the dark.

The satellite reception was hindered, so I popped in a DVD of *Pretty Woman* and microwaved a bag of popcorn. The movie made me think of Lara Reynolds, though, so I quickly swapped it out for *You've Got Mail*. I was a third of the way in when Justin called.

"I just wanted to see how you're fairing the weather," he said. "Is Duke protecting you?"

I chuckled, "Actually, he's afraid of thunder, so I'm protecting him." I looked down at the massive animal cowering next to me and softly petted him.

"I can come over and protect you both," he suggested.

I sighed, "We're okay, but we thank you for the offer. I think we're just going to head to bed."

"Oh, well then I should definitely come over," he flirted.

"Good night, Justin. Sleep well in your own bed," I replied and hung up before he could talk me into it.

I turned off the TV and checked the alarm before turning in for the night. Holding Duke close, I fell asleep as soon as I closed my eyes.

CHAPTER 26

WHEN THE ALARM woke me up on Monday, it was still pouring down rain, so I had to dry Duke off when he came inside from his potty. Of course, it was after he shook off first, spraying water all over me and the kitchen.

"I guess I should have seen that coming," I laughed and wiped the droplets off my face.

I fluffed him up and mopped up the floor with the towel before feeding us both. When I was just about ready to leave, Justin called.

"What are you doing for lunch today?" he asked with a lilt in his voice.

"I'll be working through lunch today I imagine," I answered. "There was another body found yesterday, and we're knocking on doors today."

"Oh," his voice fell, "I haven't heard about that yet, but I've not been watching the news. Since you'll be busy, though, can I take you to dinner?"

After the kind of day I was expecting to have, seeing him wouldn't necessarily be a bad thing. "If you want to drop by with a pizza around 6:30, I won't say no, but I won't feel up to going out."

"I'll see you at 6:30 then. Try to have a good day." He said goodbye, and we hung up.

I weaved through the thick traffic on Lindell Boulevard and arrived at SLCPD thirty-eight minutes later. Shortly after, the FBI agents showed up, and we split up to knock on doors while the agents stayed behind to handle our warrant requests.

We drove back to Wildwood while the fellas returned to Ellisville. Again, we went to the police station, and after apologizing to Chief Meyer for just taking off the other day, he rounded up some officers to help us. He sent Officer Jack Fisk with us to make sure everything was above board since we were out of our jurisdiction. We started at the top of our list of properties with special permits or with outbuildings.

No one answered the door on the first two homes. "Must be at work," Jack observed.

"Or afraid to open the door to the cops," I theorized.

He shrugged. "I don't think so around here, but I guess you never know."

A middle-aged woman opened the door on the third home, and we explained that we wanted to examine her outbuilding. If we did find walk-in coolers in the homes, we could easily get a warrant to search the entire premises.

She looked past us and wrung her hands. "I don't know. My husband isn't here."

I spoke up. "Ma'am, what do you keep in the building?"

"Oh, the lawnmower, gardening tools, and such. It's really a mess. What are you looking for that you'd want to search it?"

"We're looking for walk-in coolers in the area. Do you know anybody that has one?" I inquired.

She shook her head, and confusion settled in her eyes. "No, just restaurants would have freezers that large as far as I know."

"Sometimes, hunters and farmers have them to store meat," Jack told her.

"Well, I guess I'll show it to you," she finally relented and walked with us to the locked building. She was correct about its contents and about it being messy.

"Thank you for your time, ma'am," I told her, and we saw our way off her property. In the car, I added that we were likely looking for a single man. "I can't imagine even a woman in an abusive home who would put up with what he's doing."

"Well, that might explain the lack of sexual abuse, though," Marisol suggested. "Maybe his wife lets him do it as long as he's faithful to her. It could be a couple we're looking for, which would help to explain why the victims are both male and female."

"That's twisted, so you might be right," I sighed. "Let's keep checking everywhere then." I stared out the passenger window of the patrol car. "Do you think the outbuilding would be cold to the touch? We might want to just check that out on the properties where no one answers the door."

"Makes sense to me," Marisol replied. "Should we circle back to the first two homes then?"

Without answering, the officer made a U-turn and headed back to the first house. The outbuilding was warm to the touch, so I crossed the address off our list. Then we went to the second address, which was on Rockwood Trail Court. The building there was also warm to the touch.

"Well, we can dismiss this one too," Marisol observed. "I think I'll call Liam and see how they are making out."

While she made the phone call, we drove to the next address near that area. This time, a man in his twenties or thirties answered the door. The home only had a small shed on the grounds, but he had a special permit for building onto the home.

My first observation was that he was within our target age range. I noticed he had no defensive wounds, but if our killer was knocking his victims out and then cuffing them to walls or beams, as we saw in the photograph he'd left, he probably wouldn't have them. Our killer was a dominant person, so when Rick Miller didn't agree to us looking around, I deliberately pressed his buttons to see how he'd react.

"Do you have something you don't want us to see in there? I mean, we won't take long, and we're not going to go through your things, so what's the big deal?" I questioned.

"The big deal, officer, is that I have a right to my privacy, and I'm not going to let you infringe on it. On the other hand, if you want to search my body, I could live with that." He licked his thin lips, making my stomach turn.

I couldn't resist. "Officer, pat him down please."

Fisk shot me an inquisitive look at the same time Miller jumped backward.

"Please just get off my property," he exclaimed. "I have to get ready for work."

I listened intently for any sounds that would give him away, and I heard something suspicious coming from the basement.

"Who's in your basement, Mr. Miller? I hear something clanging," I told him, and it was hard to keep my voice and temper steady. I wanted to knock him aside and barge in.

He threw a glance over his shoulder at the cellar door and replied, "My cousin is down there looking at my hot water heater for me. He's a plumber."

I looked back at the truck we'd pulled up behind. It lacked advertising. "Is that his truck?"

"Yeah, why?" he wondered.

"It doesn't have a company name on it," I stated. "I would think he'd advertise."

He cracked his knuckles and stared into my eyes. "It ain't his company. He just works for the dude."

Could be valid, but it could be something else...

"All right, Mr. Miller, we'll be back later with a warrant." I turned to walk back to the car, hoping he'd change his mind and let us in, but it didn't happen.

I called Agent Pullum and requested the search warrant. "What cause do you have?" he asked.

"He fits part of our profile. He's the right age, white, has the permit for home improvement, and I heard something coming from downstairs that could be the clanging of metal cuffs. He wouldn't let us look, though. He comes off as dominant, which is another part of our killer's profile."

There was a brief silence, and then the agent told me, "All right. I'll see what I can do."

Marisol finally reached Liam and found out they didn't have any suspects yet. We went to two other houses that allowed us entry before our warrant came through. The K-9 unit and three more officers met us back at Rick Miller's address. The plumber's truck was gone.

I felt hopeful when he answered the door. "I thought you had to go to work, Mr. Miller," I taunted.

He looked at the horde of officers and the dogs wanting to search his home, and his eyes widened. "I called in sick. I have a migraine now. What are you doing back here?"

I held up the warrant that had been faxed to the Wildwood station. "We have a warrant, so step aside."

We ransacked the cellar first, but we didn't find anything. There weren't any shackles mounted in the walls or beams, and there weren't any holes to suggest that they had been at one time. The dogs didn't pick up the scent of blood, but as we drew closer toward the attached garage, they did pick up the scent of drugs. We stumbled upon cartons of meth and paraphernalia to form a meth production lab.

While our murder case wasn't solved, I was still glad to bring the cocky bastard to justice on the drug charges.

We hit a brick wall with the rest of the afternoon. Some people, who had dwelling improvements, weren't home, so we'd have to go back tomorrow. Liam and Eric had a few more to check out as well.

I was glad when it was quitting time, but then I remembered Justin was coming over, and my feelings were jumbled.

CHAPTER 27

JUSTIN SHOWED UP promptly at 6:30 with a hot pepperoni pizza, and we sat down to eat in front of the TV. I figured we wouldn't have to talk about work, us, or anything else with a show on in the background, so I put on re-runs of *Friends*. It didn't work, however.

"How's work going?" he asked in between bites.

I glanced over at him. "I really don't want to think about the job when I'm here. This is my oasis away from the madness, so please respect that."

His eyes widened. "It sounds like you're tense. I can rub your back for you. You always liked my massages," he reminded me.

"You have tough cases. You know how it feels," I sighed. "In fact, after we catch the psycho, it will be your case."

I tossed my pizza crust to Duke who was staring at me and licking his chops. I couldn't say no to his face. After dinner, I lay on the sofa and let Justin give me one of his famous massages. It felt amazing to have the tension worked out of my muscles. When I sat upright, he tried to take it to the bedroom, but I told him I needed to call it a night.

"Why are you pushing me away?" he wondered and squeezed my hand.

"Because it gets too complicated, and I can't handle it right now. Don't push." I stood and gestured toward the door. "Thanks for dinner, though."

"My pleasure. Good-night then." He gave Duke a pat on the head and showed himself out.

I locked the door, set the alarm, and dragged my tired ass off to bed. I felt mentally and physically drained, and it didn't take long to fall asleep into awful dreams.

I was back at Rick Miller's house. This time, when we searched the basement, we found metal cuffs hanging from the wall. They were processed for blood and epithelial cells but came up clean. We checked the floor out too, but no trace was found anywhere. I could hear him laughing upstairs, and it made my skin crawl. The bastard knew we wouldn't find anything.

I turned toward Liam. "Do you think he used bleach to clean up?"

He nodded. "Yes, the luminol isn't detecting anything, so it's possible he used oxygen bleach to clean it up. Regular chlorine bleach would still pop positive. Unfortunately, we don't have anything to charge him." He motioned for everyone to pack up. "Let's get out of here."

I yelled out in my sleep and sprang up in bed with sweat running down my body.

"No, we're not going to lose this case," I promised myself aloud.

I knew I wouldn't fall back to sleep, even though it was only 3:30, so I got up and made espresso and sat down to pour over my forensics books.

CHAPTER 28

IT WAS EARLY in the morning, and he watched the curator bustle around her house, getting ready for work. He had to stay out of sight from the neighbors, passersby, and of course, her husband. It was all part of his game, though. He liked the challenge. It just proved how much smarter he was than everyone else.

He ducked behind some thick shrubs when her husband came out the front door. The large man was completely oblivious to him and quickly backed down the driveway. Now was his chance, and he didn't waste a minute of it. He knocked lightly on the front door and was greeted by their yapping small poodle.

"Did you forget your keys again?" Tiffany Clark hollered. Her eyes bugged out when she opened the door and saw him standing there. "Mr. Peirick, what are you doing here? This is highly unortho—"

He cut her off quickly. She didn't even have time to scream when she saw him pull out the taser. She crumpled to the floor in front of her useless yapping dog.

He carried her to the garage and put her in the passenger seat of her car. Then he climbed into the driver's seat and opened the garage door to back out and head home. He'd already covered her mouth with chloroform to make sure she remained out cold.

He was on North Tucker Boulevard, minding the speed limit, when red and blue flashing lights lit up behind him. He pulled his hat down over his eyes and slowly pulled over, assuming the cop would drive on by. He didn't, however. He pulled up behind Mrs. Clark's Volvo.

His heart pounded fiercely in his ears as the officer approached. Cold sweat beaded on his forehead and stung his eyes when it dripped. He wiped the rest away just as the officer made it to his window.

"Good morning. I pulled you over because you have a taillight out. May I see your license and registration, please?" He noticed the sleeping woman then, and his brows pulled together. "What's wrong with her?"

"My wife has a hangover this morning, so I picked her up from work. We're just headed home," he lied and let his hand slip toward the taser in his pocket while he pretended to dig for his wallet.

"Well, you need to get that looked at as soon as you can for your safety. I won't cite you, but I still need to see your—"

A loud page from his CB radio cut him off, and he pressed the button on his attached microphone. "Officer five-six-two responding," he announced. "Get that fixed!" he shouted while running back to his patrol car. He quickly sped off into traffic with his sirens blaring.

He looked over at the sleeping woman. "That was close, wasn't it?" he asked while patting her knee. She didn't even stir, and he hoped he didn't overdose her with the chloroform. That would be no fun for him. "Come on, honey. Let's get you home. I think Tamara is lonely."

CHAPTER 29

BUZZING ON FOUR espressos, I made it to SLCPD before the others. Captain Roman approached my desk when he noticed me.

"You're in early," he observed. "Couldn't sleep?"

I looked up from my notes and charts. "Nope. I've been up since 3:30. I've read over every criminology and forensic book I have trying to figure this clown out. Someone has to pay, Boss."

He smiled and tapped his fingers on my desk. "I knew I hired you for a reason. You always did get things done down in the Drug Unit. I'm sure we can all benefit from your dedication to the job."

I felt myself blush from the compliment. "Well, thank you, and I hope I don't let you or the team down."

"I'm sure you won't. Now, I need to go update the chief of police, so I'll check with you all in a bit. Keep up the good work and show the FBI how it's done."

It would be nice if the FBI agents were being of real assistance.

The elevator chimed, and the others stepped off. I cringed when Eric handed me my coffee.

"What's that look about?" he laughed.

I smiled. "Let's just say I've had a lot of coffee this morning."

"That's good because you're going to need it," Liam mumbled. "We have to finish knocking on doors and hopefully turn something up this time."

"When we're finished in Wildwood, we'll go on to Eureka," Marisol offered, and he nodded in approval.

"Right, and we'll go to Town and Country, but if we don't turn anything up, then I don't know where we'll look next," he replied with a disgusted sigh.

"We're going with you today," Agent Pullum announced when he stepped around the corner. "Agent Gould will go with the ladies, and I'll go with you gentlemen. Agent Amos got called back to the office on another case."

Great. Big Sister will be watching.

Since Agent Gould was with us, we didn't need the local police for jurisdiction, but Officer Fisk knew the roads, so we met him at the station and piled into his patrol car. "Since we've got a full car, I'll have to call for back-up if we need to bring someone in."

Agent Gould mumbled, "With this guy, you're going to need it anyway." I couldn't help but think she was probably right.

We went back to each house we'd tried yesterday that didn't have someone home, and we got lucky on the first two houses. No one answered at the third house, so we walked around the perimeter, looking in through the basement windows. We didn't see anything out of the ordinary, and it was the last one on our list, so we went back to our car at the station and left for Eureka.

We met with Chief Thomas, and she set us up with Officer Terri Devos, who was more than happy to assist. "I've been watching this story develop on the news, and I wanted to be able to help," she gushed.

"We'll take all the help we can get," I mentioned, and Marisol enthusiastically nodded in agreement.

We started at the closest address and searched the property with the owner's permission. The man was surprised to see us but cooperative, which made me think he wasn't our guy before we even started looking around. His outbuilding was a storage shed for his riding lawnmower and lawn maintenance supplies, and the extra amenity to the home was another guest room he'd added on. We thanked him for his cooperation and went to the next address. No one was home, so we peeked in the windows. It was too difficult to see much, though, because of thick black curtains. We marked that address as one to come back to. The other homes were cleared.

"There are some wooded areas in Parkdale too," Officer Devos mentioned. "And it's near here. Do you want to check it out?"

Marisol answered for us. "Yes, let's go have a look and see if anything turns up. Although, we don't have a printout of the houses to look at, so we'll just have to drive around to look for outbuildings. That won't help with special permits, though."

"That's fine. I'm on the clock," the officer laughed.

I called Eric to see if they were having any luck, and he said they had a few houses to circle back to; otherwise, nothing struck them as out of the ordinary yet. I told him we were going to check Parkdale and then head back to SLCPD. Then I called the Jefferson County Assessor's Office and spoke to a clerk in Real Property. I explained the situation and requested a list of properties with the modifications and outbuildings to be emailed to me. She was reluctant, so I put Agent Gould on the line with her, and that did the trick. I had the list in my inbox within a few minutes. Fortunately, there weren't that many.

I plugged the first address into my GPS locator, and we were on our way. The home was inhabited by an elderly couple, who had built on an entertainment room for their grandchildren. We took their word for it and went to the next address. No one was home, and the basement windows were covered by thick curtains, so we'd have to circle back to it. We went to the next two, cleared them, and then went back to the questionable one. No one was home yet, so it was time to call it quits. We went back to the Eureka Police Department, and Chief Thomas said she'd contact the Jefferson County Sheriff's Office on the Parkdale address we needed to check out yet, and she'd revisit the one house in Eureka too.

The guys had a few homes in Town and Country that required another visit also. Two had outbuildings, while the other had a special building permit for an attachment.

"Did you touch the outbuildings to see if they were cold?" I asked them.

Eric blushed. "No, but I suppose that would've been a good idea."

I chuckled at him. "Hindsight is twenty-twenty, right?"

"Yep." He looked at his watch. "It's quitting time I suppose, or is there something else for today, Boss?" he asked Captain Roman.

"No, go home and get your rest. Tomorrow, we need to come up with a plan B," he replied.

CHAPTER 30

HIS HEART POUNDED for five minutes after the police left his property. Detective Delossa was even lovelier in person, and it made him want to adjust his portrait of her. However, he had other concerns to worry about. For one thing, how the hell did they find his home? What made them want to look there? His neighbors were miles away, so he knew they hadn't seen or heard anything suspicious. He had the strong feeling they'd be back, too, so how would he handle that?

An idea came to him, and he went to the garage to grab some wood for a sign. He hammered a post onto a piece of paneling and then took it to his studio to paint it with a fake realty listing. Once it dried, he'd put it in the yard to throw the authorities off. Why would they suspect a home that has people looking inside it every day?

I'm such a genius.

He heard rattling in the basement and figured his newest guest was alert. He couldn't wait to welcome her to the fun, so he hurried down the stairs.

Tiffany Clark looked up at him in confusion. "Mr. Peirick, what the hell is going on here?" she demanded.

With a low chuckle, he removed the sheet he'd hung up in front of her, so she could see his other guest, Tamara. Her jaw went slack and fell open as far as it could. Then she began to scream. He laughed at first but then worried the cops could be back at any moment, so he fetched the duct tape.

"Why are you doing—" her words were cut off into a muffle as the tape covered her mouth.

He laughed again and stared into her eyes with daggers. "Why am I doing this? Because I can is the simplest answer, but it's really because you rejected my hard work, so now you get to become a part of it." He held up his masterpiece of the dead hooker. "Lovely, isn't it?"

Her eyes pooled with tears as reality overcame her. Between the woman on the opposite wall, who had dried blood all over her, and the terrifying painting, she knew the fate that was in store for her.

"You told me to show emotion in my work, so I chose to use fear and suffering. I did a terrific job too if I do say so myself"—he gestured to the painting—"Yes, she suffered a lot for me, and I perfectly captured the moments." He picked up his camera and snapped some pictures of her distress. "I think you're going to make a wonderful model," he growled with a threatening glare. "And now that I have seen your fear, I need to see your pain." He approached her with a hammer and nail.

CHAPTER 31

I PICKED UP a bottle of Kahlúa on the way home and made a mudslide as soon as I walked in through the door. I didn't drink often, but it was one of those days when a drink sounded good. If we came up empty on the properties that needed searching yet, I just didn't know what we'd do. The captain had said something about a plan B, but did he have one already? I know I didn't.

"You're not alone in this. Rely on your team, Delossa," I chastised myself.

My phone rang, and it was Maria Gomez. I hoped she had some useful information for my case.

"Hi, Maria. What's up?" I wondered.

Her voice was in a whisper, so I knew she wasn't alone. "You're in danger. The word on the street is the Bloods are looking for you hardcore. They even threatened to start killing at random to flush you out."

I blew out a rush of air. This was all I needed to deal with right now. "Thank you. I'll heed your warning. Have you heard anything regarding the Slasher case?" I figured I might as well ask while I had her on the phone.

"No, not yet. I'll keep listening and watching, though," she answered.

"Thanks. Call me anytime," I told her and hung up.

I fixed another mudslide and stepped out onto the back patio to watch the sun go down while Duke played in the yard. My phone rang again, and my breath caught in my throat when I saw it was Liam.

"Hello?" I answered the call. "What bad news do you have for me now?"

"Well, you don't have to come in again, but I do have some news. The curator for the City Museum has been reported missing by her husband. She didn't show up for work today, and she never made it home either, but her car is gone. I just wanted to let you know."

I closed my eyes and willed the day to be over. "Are you sure you don't need me to come in?"

"No, you're fine. None of us are going back in, but Missing Persons is working on it. They are out searching with the dogs. We'll discuss it more in the morning," he said.

"Okay. I'll see you then. Bye." I hung up and stared off into the distance. *When will this be over?*

Feeling the effects of the alcohol and the stress of the case, I took a relaxing bath and headed to bed early without supper. Curling up with Duke was just what I needed to feel better.

CHAPTER 32

I WOKE UP an hour and forty-five minutes early on Wednesday and thought about going for a run with Duke, but then I remembered Maria's warning about the Bloods, and after the encounter I had on Saturday, I decided to use my StairMaster instead. Being on the force was dangerous regardless, but perhaps while the Slasher case was active, it wouldn't hurt to be extra vigilant.

I had my stereo on and almost didn't hear my phone ring half-way into my workout. It was Maria calling again.

As soon as I said hello, she rattled off, "I can't talk long, but I wanted to tell you to be careful today. I think something is going to go down, but I'm not sure when or where. I just heard them saying that today is the day."

"Okay, thanks for calling. I'll notify the Gang Unit, so they can keep an eye out for unusual activity," I replied.

"Cool. See ya." The line went dead.

I showered after the call, quickly ate, and then headed in early, so I'd have time to talk to the Gang Unit before starting my day. I relayed Maria's message, and they promised to be extra watchful of the gang's activities. I also told my partners, and they agreed to have my back too. I felt confident around them, but what about when I went home? I had an alarm, a big dog, and of course, my gun, but I didn't want to be alone. I supposed I could always ask Justin to stay over. Then again, he didn't believe in guns or fighting, so I wasn't sure if he would do any good if I was attacked.

"So, I called you all last night about the curator's disappearance, and there is no word on her yet," Liam began, snapping me out of my reverie. "Tiffany Clark's husband, Ron, saw her in the morning before he left for work, and no one has seen or heard from her since."

"Has the CSU been to her house to check for evidence?" I wondered, thinking maybe she was abducted from her home. "Did the Clarks have any maintenance men coming over yesterday or anything of that nature, and have the neighbors been interrogated?"

Liam answered, "Yes, the technicians have been there, but they didn't recover any trace. No one was expected to be stopping by, and the neighbors didn't see anyone suspicious in the neighborhood. So, I think she might have stopped someplace on the way to the museum and was taken from there, but no witnesses have come forward."

"Let's map out the route she normally takes from home to work and see what coffee shops and gas stations are along the way," Marisol suggested and lit up the LED map we had of the St. Louis area.

Liam used an LED pin and marked the street she lived on—Spruce Street. Then he put a pin where the City Museum is, which turned out to be only a handful of miles from her house.

"So, she'd take Spruce to North Tucker Boulevard to Lucas Avenue," Eric pointed out and then typed something into his computer. "The closest coffee shop is the Washington Avenue Post on Washington Avenue."

I lit up spots on the map. "Or she could've stopped at Kaldi's Coffee here on Chestnut Street, and there's also Shell gas station on North Tucker and Mobil on North Thirteenth Street in the area. We could contact them for surveillance footage."

Liam picked up his desk phone and began dialing. "I'll have Missing Persons do it. We have to focus on our killer's motives and think about where he'll strike next."

I ran my hands through my long hair with a heavy sigh. "Therein lies the problem. Nothing ties our victims together yet, so we have no idea where he'll strike next."

"I agree that so far the victims look random, but there has to be something about them that makes him choose them," Liam countered. "That's what we need to figure out."

A knock on the doorframe stopped him from elaborating further. It was a FedEx driver with a package.

"I'm looking for an Agent Sasha Delossa," he announced, and I raised my hand. I signed for the package and thanked him, but I was confused because I hadn't ordered anything. I let the package rest on my desk without touching it.

Once he was out of earshot, I told the others, "I haven't ordered anything. We need to get the Bomb Squad up here."

I slowly backed away from my desk, and Liam pushed the alarm button to evacuate the building. We all knew a bomb could be remotely detonated once it was in the hands of the recipient. Since packages can be tracked online, the sender could even use the FedEx system to see that it had been signed for.

"Did you see who it was from?" Eric asked when we were outside in the crowd.

I nodded. "I glanced at the name, which I don't recognize. It said it was sent from a Jimmy Sutton. I didn't check the address."

"That's okay, we'll look at it later. I told the technicians where the package is, and there they are now," Liam stated and pointed to the men in dark blue protective gear who were rushing into the building.

We held our breaths for several minutes until the supervising technician yelled that the building was cleared. Relief washed over me, but I was still confused. Who was Jimmy Sutton, and why was he sending me something? Was it simply a ploy to get me out of the building? Police personnel surrounded me, so it didn't make sense for the Bloods to try something with us all out there, and I highly doubted they had a sharpshooter on a rooftop nearby. The St. Louis Slasher, though, was another story. *But why would he target me?* The eerie phone call ran through my mind.

When we reached the door, the supervising technician told Liam, "It's a flat non-electrical object."

"Thank you for checking it out," Liam responded, and I added my own thanks on top. Then we rushed upstairs.

They stared at me while I tried to open the package with my trembling hands. "It says it's from Jimmy Sutton, of Two-Eleven Cass Avenue"—I looked up into their expectant faces—"I still have no idea who that is."

Eric was inputting the name and address into his computer while I pulled out the contents of the box. It was a painting—specifically, it was a painted portrait of me.

"He apparently knows who *you* are," Marisol observed. "Eric, what did you find?"

My hands grew clammy, so I set the artwork down on my desk and looked at Eric for his response. "There is no such address, but there are a few James Suttons. One lives in Kirkwood, one lives here in St. Louis, and another is in Maryland Heights. Of course, if I extend the search, I'm sure we'll find more," he said.

The captain had been listening in and watching, so he advised us, "Go knock on doors while the crime lab takes a look at the painting."

Instead of getting up to leave, I started tapping on my computer, drawing their collective attention.

"What are you doing?" Marisol wondered.

I glanced up at her. "I'm trying to cross-reference artists with the name to see if there are any in the area. That's hardly a paint by number, and the artist has definite talent." Sadly, the search came up null.

"Ready to go?" Liam inquired, and I nodded.

"Yep. Let's see what turns up," I answered with a sick feeling in my stomach. It was highly probable that the name was fake too.

CHAPTER 33

HE RUBBED HIS hands together while he stared at his computer screen. The painting had been delivered. He studied the loopy lines of her signature. It was feminine but confident. It was artistic. He wondered if she liked it, and he wondered if she was looking for Jimmy Sutton yet. The payback to the college art teacher would be epic. The teacher had never believed he could amount to anything with his artistic passion, which is why he'd gone in another direction with his line of work. Well, he'd prove the asshole wrong just as he'd soon prove the bitch in the basement wrong. Speaking of which...

He trotted down the stairs, whistling a joyful tune, and approached the curator who was still crying. He was sure part of it was from the nail he'd driven into her left hand.

"Does that still hurt?" he mocked, and she tried to shake her head up and down, but she was too weak. He held up his camera and mumbled, "Let's capture your misery for all to see." He snapped three photos and then looked back over them with a frown. "I don't think it's powerful enough. You've got to really own it. Pretend you're in a movie and work it." He grabbed another nail and pounded it into her right hand this time. Her eyes squeezed shut, and muffled screams escaped around the tape. "That's better! Look at you!" He took more photos and strolled over to the other woman. "Don't worry, Tamara, I haven't forgotten you, but I don't want to repeat myself too much. I have to keep the police guessing."

He gave her a sip of water from the bottle before puncturing a hole into her forearm with a power drill. Her eyes rolled back into her head, and her body violently shook. The jerking stopped within minutes, though, and only glassy eyes stared back at him. *Click. Click.*

CHAPTER 34

ONE HUNDRED COLE Street in the city was our first stop. Mrs. Cole answered the door and said her husband, who was a cardiologist at St. Louis Children's Hospital, wouldn't be home until after 9:00. She wanted, of course, to know what our visit was about, so I asked if he had any artistic hobbies. She laughed and told us he didn't have a creative bone in his body, so we crossed him off the list.

We went to Thirteen East Jefferson Avenue in Kirkwood next, and a portly older man answered. "Can I help you?" he asked when we flashed our badges and introduced ourselves.

"Are you James Sutton?" I inquired, and he slowly nodded.

"Yes, I'm James. What do you need, officers?" His voice trembled, and I immediately presumed he wasn't our confident, narcissistic killer. He just didn't fit our profile.

"May we come in?" I asked, and he let us inside and led us to his living room. "James, I received a painting today, and I'm just trying to find out who it came from," I told the man. "Would you know anything about that?"

His face scrunched tight. "I have no idea what you're talking about, officer." He pulled out a handkerchief and dabbed his face.

"It's Detective Delossa," I corrected him. "Do you like to paint, James? Did you do this?" I held up my phone to show him a photo of the painting.

"I didn't do that, but the likeness is quite good. I've not picked up paints in months; however, I suppose…" His voice trailed off.

"You suppose what?" Eric demanded.

"I suppose it could be from one of my students," James finished.

"Your students?" I inquired.

He smiled. "Yes, I teach art at the St. Louis Community College. I have for nearly fifteen years now." He looked closer at the photo. "Why did you think I did that?"

"Your name was on the return address," Liam announced, and the man's face lost all its color.

"Well, I can only guess that one of my students is playing a hoax on me then, but I assure you I didn't do that. For one thing, I'd never use just one color. I know Picasso had a blue period, but I'm not one for doing that sort of thing. I do, however, have a female student who likes to paint black and whites. I can always ask her about it if you want."

I looked at the others and used my eyes to convey my thoughts. This wasn't our guy, and the female student wasn't either.

"That won't be necessary, but we thank you for your time," Liam told him and shook his hand to give him a business card. "If you do think of something or hear something about it, though, please don't hesitate to call us."

"Sure, but can I ask what it has to do with?" he wondered.

"We aren't sure yet," I answered him, and we left his home.

In the car, I had to ask, "Are we sure we aren't chasing our tails on this? That old guy was probably right about being set up by a student."

Marisol interjected, "Our killer might be one of his students or even a former student. That's where we should look."

Liam was quiet for a minute, but he didn't start the car. Finally, he said, "Sasha, go back up there and see what we have to do to get his class roster."

"You bet," I chirped and hopped out of the car. Mr. Sutton was apparently watching us from the window because he opened the door before I got there.

"What else can I do for you *Detective*?" he called out.

"We'd like a copy of your class roster, Mr. Sutton. Can you get that for me?" I questioned.

He dabbed his face again. "I'm not sure about the school's policy on something like that, so I think it's best if you ask them. You'll have my full cooperation as long as it's okay with them."

I nodded. "Fair enough. That's what we'll do then. Have a good day." I went back to the car, and we headed for home.

"How do we even know that the painting is related to the Slasher case?" Marisol asked when we got to our desks.

Chris's voice rang out as he stepped into the office with papers in hand. "Because the medium for the painting is blood mixed with red paint, and the DNA matches your victims."

The world stopped spinning, but the room didn't, and I fell into my chair. Shit just got real.

"What the hell kind of personal message is that to me then? What does it mean?" I mumbled aloud.

"Well, I think it means we need to get a psychologist's opinion or someone who can interpret art anyway," Liam suggested. "There must be something the Slasher wants us to see."

I shrugged. "Sure. I'll take any help we can get. This shit has to end, preferably with my neck still intact."

I slumped with my head in my hands while the case weighed heavily on my shoulders. How did this freakshow get fixated on me? Was I his next intended victim? *To hell with that notion.*

I read over the lab's findings. There were no prints, no hairs, and no fibers. There was only the victims' DNA. Five different strands of DNA, including that of missing Tamara Boyd. I scribbled one word on my blotter—*why?*

The captain rounded the corner and told us we could all go home early. "I have a feeling you'll be called back in at any given minute, so rest while you can." His somber tone did nothing to boost our morale, but we knew he was right. This killer was nowhere near his endgame. I could feel it in my bones.

CHAPTER 35

WHEN I DROVE home, I kept my eye on the rearview mirror to make sure I wasn't being followed, and I examined everyone walking along the sidewalk to make sure they weren't staring too hard at me. I felt eyes on me from every direction, which was a reasonable assumption considering how large the Bloods gang is.

"You have plenty of ammo at home if you need it," I reminded myself. I intended to dig out my Mace and taser too.

Duke was happy to see me like always, and that made me smile. I gave him more food and fresh water before considering my own meal. I wasn't that hungry despite missing lunch today and dinner last night, so I made do with a TV dinner from the freezer.

While I ate the crappy meal, I thought about the killer's victims who weren't being fed at all while he tortured them for days. I had no idea how they were strong enough to hold on. I couldn't imagine them *wanting* to hold on only to endure more pain. For the first time, I cried hard for the victims.

A loud shot rang outside my house, making me run to the living room window with my Glock drawn. It was just Mr. Anderson's classic car backfiring as it puttered down the street. It always did that, and it caught me off guard every time. Duke was growling and barking at the front door, so I soothed him.

"It's all right, baby. It's just our crazy neighbors."

My cell phone rang, and it was Justin again. "I just wanted to look in on you," he greeted me.

"Unless Mr. Anderson's old Chevy gets me, I think I'll be all right," I replied with a giggle.

"I don't get it," he mumbled. "What does a car have to do with your well-being?"

I laughed again. "The car backfired and scared the bejesus out of me."

"Oh, I see. That's funny. Since you're on edge, would you like some company tonight?" he inquired.

I gave the invitation careful consideration. "Well, let me ask you something. What would you do if I needed rescuing? Would you throw a legal document at them, hoping to inflict a papercut?" I teased.

He sighed, and I could picture his scowl. "It might surprise you to know that I own a gun as well. I used to hunt with my dad when I was younger, and since we live in the big, bad city, I decided to keep it on hand."

"Hmm…I feel safer already," I joked. "If you want to come over, you can, but your jammies stay on."

"And I suppose the dog sleeps next to you. Am I right?" he wondered.

"You bet he does. Can you handle that?" I reached over Duke, throwing his tennis ball for him, which he quickly plodded after.

"I suppose so. Is that Thunder Paws now? I can hear him running around," he chuckled.

"We're playing, but you can come over anyway. I'll see you soon. Bye." I disconnected the line and tidied up my dinner mess.

Before he came over, I wanted to check up on Denise, so I quickly called her.

She answered after one ring and asked, "Are you checking up on your little sister again?"

I smiled to myself. "Someone has to keep an eye on you. Is everything okay?"

She let out a disgusted sigh. "Yes, Sasha, everything is fine and dandy. Well, Marcus is out of town for a work conference, and I miss him, but everything else is fine."

I bit my lip, contemplating her situation. I was worried about her being alone. Marcus would lay down his life for her, but he wasn't home, so I had to step up. "Why don't you come over and stay with us until he gets back? I'd feel better if you had someone to watch over you."

"Sasha, I'm twenty-five years old and able to handle myself. You can't protect me forever, and you aren't the only one who inherited the tough genes from the Delossa family tree," she ranted.

I rolled my eyes. "I am the only one with a gun and a two-hundred-pound dog, though."

"Oh, that's right! You got a dog. I'll be right over." She hung up before I could warn her that Justin would be here too.

I looked down at Duke, who was waiting for me to throw the ball again. "I just found Aunt Denise's price. I guess we're going to have two guests tonight."

Fifteen minutes passed before the first door chime. I knew without looking it was Justin because he lived closer than Denise. As soon as he stepped inside, Duke quit barking and jumped on him, sniffing him all over.

"What is he doing?" he laughed.

"He's seeing if you have been faithful to him. Have you been petting other dogs?" I questioned with a raised brow.

"Not that I'm aware of, but I think I might sleepwalk, especially after today." He dragged his hand across his forehead and made a whooshing sound.

"Why? What happened to you today?" I inquired.

He sat on the sofa, so I sat across from him in my armchair, so we could talk face to face. "I'm just involved with a tough case. We have a woman who killed her husband in what she claims was self-defense, but there's no proof of abuse in the home. The prosecutor wants to send her up the river, but I disagree. She seems mentally bashed to me and would benefit more from a mental hospital than a prison."

I cocked my head at him. "That surprises me. I always saw you as thinking everything was black and white."

He shrugged his slender shoulders. "I think there are three sides to every triangle."

I laughed at his remark and then jumped when Duke ran to the door, barking and growling.

"What the hell is wrong with him?" Justin asked before we heard the knock.

"By the way, my sister is staying over," I chirped and walked to the door, pushing Duke aside. "It's okay, big boy. It's just Aunt Denise," I cooed.

"Do you really think you need a babysitter to protect you from me?" he inquired with a half-smile.

I opened the door to let her in, telling him, "No, I just need my bodyguard."

Denise ignored Justin and went straight for the dog after dropping her overnight bag. "Hi, puppy," she chimed and hugged on him. "What's your name?"

I lowered my voice and replied, "I'm Duke."

She looked up, laughing, and noticed Justin standing there with his hands in his pockets. They'd met before, so I didn't need to do introductions.

"I didn't know you were going to be here, Justin," she remarked.

"Likewise"—he looked down at the sofa—"Do you have blankets for this thing?" he asked me.

"If you two lovebirds want to share a bed, I can sleep on the couch and wear earplugs," she teased.

I wagged my index finger at her and then headed to the linen closet. I pulled out a blanket and pillow for him. "They aren't Egyptian cotton like you're used to, sir, but I imagine they'll do," I told him in a haughty voice.

He sighed playfully. "I'll manage."

Before long, I set the security alarm, and we all said goodnight. Denise, Duke, and I headed off to my room, while Justin planted himself on the sofa. I couldn't tell who was kicking me more, her or the dog, but eventually, dreams overcame me.

CHAPTER 36

HE FELT TOO tired to paint, but the creative juices were still flowing, so he picked up his sketch pad and pencil and sketched another lovely portrait of Detective Sasha Delossa. This one he'd keep for himself, though. He drew her chained to his basement wall, pleading for him to stop hurting her. He drew her broken and surrendering to his will. He expressed pain on her face along with disbelief, fear, and failure. She had failed to catch him, so he caught her instead.

He had already visited Tiffany Clark. He had peeled back the tape to allow her some water, and she had spewed obscenities at him. He laughed in response and reminded her to act like a refined lady. Then he had replaced the tape and bid her goodnight after pressing on the nail in her right hand. Her muffled cries almost engorged him, but that's not what his mission was all about.

With a self-satisfied smile, he turned out the light and dreamed about adding the good detective to his collection.

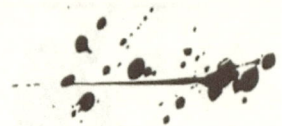

He lured the detective until she was close enough to tase, and then he slumped her flaccid body over his shoulder. He took her to his dungeon and propped her up against the wall, cuffing her wrists and ankles. This woke her up with a start, and she began screaming. He wasn't worried, though, because no one knew where to look for her. They'd already dismissed his property from their suspect pool.

She flailed violently against the restraints until he heard her left wrist snap like a twig. He wagged a finger in front of her face.

"Uh-uh. You'll only hurt yourself, and that's my job," he stated with a smug smile.

He picked up a leather cat o' nine tails that he'd purchased at a local adult store and brushed the leather fingers over her forearms.

"Don't worry, my dear. This isn't for sex. This has nothing to do with sex at all, lest you think of me as Marquis de Sade." He reared his arm back and lashed her flesh, causing her to wince and cry out in pain. "That's it! Scream for me. Scream bloody murder because that's what this is!" He lashed again but harder this time, and her cries of misery bounced off the walls.

He woke up and listened to the pounding of his heart in his ears. Sadism excited him even when in dreams. He just couldn't wait for the real deal.

CHAPTER 37

WHEN I WOKE up, Denise was already out of bed and in my shower, so I went into the kitchen to make breakfast for everyone. Justin beat me to it, however, and was cooking sausage, eggs, and toast. He also had a pot of coffee made, so I poured some into the largest mug in my collection.

"I figured you'd want coffee as soon as you got up," he stated and nudged my shoulder.

I slowly nodded while taking a sip of the strong brew. "I need a caffeine I.V. instead," I murmured. "I have the feeling today is going to be rough."

He rubbed the small of my back in circles, which he knew I loved. "Why is that? I mean besides the case you're working on, what else is going on?"

I cracked my knuckles, which was a habit I wouldn't mind breaking. "Well, since I arrested Carlos Garcia, I have the entire Bloods crew after me, but hey, no biggie, right?"

I heard the concern in his voice. "It's a huge deal, and I heard there was a bomb scare yesterday. What was that all about? Was it related to the gang?"

I took another sip of my coffee before I answered, "No, it had to do with a package I received from the St. Louis Slasher."

He did a spit take all over my clean kitchen floor. "Wait! What?"

I took a deep breath and explained to him about the portrait, including our conversation with the art professor.

He rubbed the area between his eyebrows. "So, you think that the Slasher is one of his students then?"

I looked down into my mug as if the swirling creamer in my coffee held the answers I needed. "At this point, I think he could be my neighbor with the backfiring Chevy. I just don't know about this guy."

He patted my ass. "Well, they wouldn't have hired you for the Homicide Unit if you couldn't do the job, so I have faith in you. And, when it's all over with, I say let's play hooky for a day or two and go someplace."

I laughed and fanned my face because with the stove going, my kitchen was extra warm. "I'm sure they'll give me time off after I just got the job."

He leaned down and kissed my neck. "They should because you're special."

I laughed. "You only say that because it's true."

Denise walked in and asked, "What's true? That you're a dork? We all know that."

I shot her my big sister glare before getting a mug for her out of the dishwasher. She made a disgusted face. "You know I don't drink coffee. Do you have tea?"

I fetched the tea, and breakfast was ready, so I got the plates and silverware too. We sat down together, and Duke moved in circles around the table just waiting for someone to either give him a handout or drop something.

Before I could give him a sausage link, Denise gave him one. He plopped down next to her chair, and just like that, I'd been replaced in his eyes.

Justin was the first one finished eating, and he left right after because of an early morning trial. Denise laid into me as soon as the door shut behind him.

"So, what's that all about? Are you getting back together?" she questioned with a mischievous tone.

I tilted my head and gave her a flat response. "No, we aren't reconciling. He's just a friend."

"Friend with benefits?" she teased, and I flashed back to last Thursday night. If I told her what had happened, she'd tease me relentlessly.

"No, because he'll get the wrong idea about us," I settled on.

She let out a disgusted grunt. "Guys like the no-strings-attached option. Well, most guys do."

I opened my hands up with a shrug. "He's not like most guys, so there you go. Anyway, I need to get cleaned up for work since you hogged the shower, so please just lock the door behind you when you leave and don't even think about dognapping Duke."

She looked down at my snoozing friend and frowned. "I want a dog, but Marcus is allergic."

"Dump him then," I said with a smirk.

"No way. I'll just have to have unlimited visits with Duke," she replied and rubbed the dog's belly.

I laughed all the way to the bathroom. I knew she was being perfectly serious about coming over more often because she was just as fond of dogs.

She was gone when I got out of the shower, and I quickly dressed for work. I blow-dried my hair and put it in a quick braid before slapping on some makeup and kissing Duke goodbye.

The traffic wasn't any heavier than usual, so I made it to SLCPD a few minutes early. Marisol was already sitting at her desk.

"You beat me," I pointed out with a grin.

She was studying her notes with a grim expression, but she looked up and returned my smile. "I couldn't sleep. This is really getting to me, and I didn't want to wake Joe up. He's been on nights lately, filling in for one of the supervisors on vacation."

"It can be rough when work gets in the way," I mentioned, thinking about Justin. "Between my hours and undercover work and his caseload, it just got to be too much to overcome, you know?"

She tapped her finger to her chin. "That's right, you said you dated ADA Sinclair before. He's a good-looking man."

I blushed at her compliment and looked away. "Yes, he's handsome, but he's also…complicated." I couldn't think of another word to describe him. Our relationship had been a series of fights and miscommunication smoothed over by a sultry physical connection. That's why I didn't want to go down that particular road again. "I suppose all lawyers are," I added to lighten the mood.

Eric and Liam walked in, and Eric had the coffees for us. "Did everyone get enough beauty rest?" he asked with a lopsided grin.

I couldn't resist the jab, so I narrowed my eyes at him and replied, "Well, *some* of us did."

He put his hand over his heart and feigned shock, stumbling backward and bumping into the captain.

Captain Roman scowled and cleared his throat. "I'm glad to see you're all wide awake this morning because another victim was just discovered. Tamara Boyd was dumped inside a horse carriage on Laclede's Landing. Chris is already on the way, so catch up with him, will you?"

"Right away, Boss," Liam belted, and we all rushed for the stairs.

When Marisol pulled the car up behind the flashing patrol cars, hordes of people were already piled up on the outside perimeter of the crime tape, straining to get a look at the latest thrill kill. It was disturbing how so many people got their jollies off the suffering of others. All too quickly, someone's last minutes on earth ended up as a casualty reported on the 6:00 news. It roiled my stomach.

"I'm tired of being three steps behind this lunatic," Eric spat over the noise of the crowd, and I had to agree with him whole-heartedly.

I looked over an officer's shoulder at the victim. The mangled body stared up at me with questions behind her hollow, blank eyes. "I've never seen a worse case of death," I mumbled with disgust.

Blood was caked all over her and had come from multiple gashes, including a large hole ripped into her forearm right below the tattoo of her son's name—Jayden. I couldn't spare the poor child the news of his mother's untimely demise, but I could spare him this image that would haunt him forever. I could make every attempt to keep the crime scene photos and description out of his head. Hell, I'd hide the photos if I had to. No one deserved the torment she'd suffered, and no one deserved to see it.

Chris spoke while he examined the remains. "She has the common stab wounds and burns on her feet. As you can see, though, she has the bonus torture of a hole drilled into her arm, and yes, I think he used a drill to do it. She appears malnourished and dehydrated just like the others. I also see what appears to be rodent bites on her feet. I won't know the COD until I open her up." He let us have a better look at her, and then he had the technicians take her away.

"Why is he leaving the bodies out in the open like this?" Marisol wondered. "Do you suppose it's for shock value?"

I nodded. "Probably that, and he wants to be sure someone will find them to instill fear in the community."

"We should call him the St. Louis terrorist then," she mused aloud.

We got out of the way for the CSU technicians to process the scene and followed Liam and Eric back to our cars.

"It takes an awful lot of rage to inflict pain on someone like that," I mumbled on the drive back, referring to the hole in Tamara's arm. "We should stop by her house and notify her fiancé on the way back. I have the address here in my notes."

"Sure, we can do that," she responded. "They deserve closure."

"They do, but I don't think they're going to have closure until this killer fries in the electric chair," I speculated.

She pulled into John Washington's driveway, and he walked out the front door. "Is this about Tamara?" he asked immediately when he recognized us.

"Mr. Washington, let's go inside," I suggested.

He crossed his arms over his broad chest and shook his head. "No, Jayden is in there. Tell me now."

I looked down, sensing he already knew what we had to say, and swallowed hard. "I'm sorry, but her body has been found."

"Her body?" he squawked, and tears streamed down his face. "So, she's gone then?"

"I'm sorry, sir," Marisol added.

He composed himself enough to ask a follow-up question. "Is this related to the serial killer case I heard about on the news? Did he kill my girl?"

His agonizing expression caused a shiver to run through me. "I'm afraid so, sir. We are doing everything we can to bring the person responsible to justice, and we'll let you know when we have something."

"You don't have any suspects, though. That's what they said on the news," he wailed.

"We're diligently working on it," I assured him.

He looked over his shoulder, and I followed his gaze. Their son was peeking through the curtains. "I've got to go. I have to tell Jayden his mom isn't coming home." He turned to walk away, but then he spun around and jabbed a finger at us. "You find this son-of-a-bitch, or I will," he spat.

We climbed into the car and were both silent the rest of the way back to SLCPD.

CHAPTER 38

HE DIDN'T WANT to go into work, so he called in sick. He needed to create, and he could only do that at home. He took the sketch of Detective Delossa and turned it into a vibrant painting. He used colors to make it realistic instead of using just the red. He needed more red paint anyway. He looked at the floorboards, wondering how his guest was doing. He was down to one now, so he had room for two more. One to keep Tiffany company and one for the other house. *It was time to go hunting.*

First, though, he needed to check on Tiffany. He couldn't have her dying on him until he was ready for it. He took her a meal replacement shake and ripped the tape off her mouth. She was quiet and eagerly accepted the straw.

"This will make your tummy feel better, and I promise I didn't put anything in it," he claimed, and it made her pause. She must not have cared, though, because she went ahead and finished the drink off.

He dabbed at her mouth before covering it back up with tape. He could probably leave it uncovered since he had already put the phony for sale sign in the yard, but he wanted to be certain, and he wanted to torment her for the way she'd treated him.

"How are your hands feeling today?" he asked in a voice laced with fake concern. Tears immediately streamed down her face, so he reached out and wiped one away. "Aw, don't cry. I'm going to give you something to take your mind off it because that's what my dear old dad used to do for me."

He picked the hammer up, watching her eyes widen with terror, and swung it toward her right shin. The loud snapping sound reverberated off the concrete and mixed with her muffled shrieking. He took a few photos and was about to leave when he thought it sounded like she was trying to ask him something.

He pulled the tape and inquired, "Did you have a question, dear?"

Through sobs, she managed to squeak out, "Why are you doing this to me? Is it because I didn't accept your paintings into the gallery?"

He chuckled and replaced the tape. "Your gallery should feel honored to house my masterpieces, and I'm sure it will be doing so very soon. Once they replace you, I'll take them to the next curator, and I imagine they'll have better taste than you."

He spun on his heel and left her alone to enjoy her desolation. Then he left and drove to Sunset Hills to do his hunting. They weren't expecting him there.

He parked outside the shopping plaza and scanned the pedestrians mindlessly bustling in and out of stores. They just had no idea what could rain down on them on a whim. They barely looked both ways before crossing the street, so of course, they didn't notice him. He played eeny meeny miny moe until he chose him. His next guest was a tall, lanky redheaded man, who was too busy digging in his pocket for his keys to notice the pretty blond woman checking him out. He popped his hood to draw the redhead's attention, and it worked. Men always took the bait when he lured them with car trouble. It was the macho need to prove their worth that drew them in. Every guy suddenly becomes a car expert.

"Do you need some help?" the redhead asked.

He looked over and smiled at the volunteer. "Yeah, I can't get her to turn over, and I don't know much about cars. I think it might be my ignition switch though." He pointed to the steering column.

"All right. Let me take a look at it," the other man suggested.

"Thanks. I appreciate it," he said as he climbed out of the SUV.

Once the redhead was in the driver's seat and checking the switch out, he leaned over with the taser and pressed it into the man's waist. The man wiggled and then slumped over. Making sure no one was watching, he shoved him over in the bench seat, which was a wonderful feature in his Suburban. Then he shut the hood and quickly drove away before someone saw what he was up to.

He injected the man with scopolamine before pulling into a gas station. That was the bad thing about the SUV—it was a gas hog. The redhead was slumped against the passenger door, looking like he was asleep, so no one was the wiser. He paid at the pump and filled up the tank before heading home, making sure he drove the speed limit. He couldn't risk getting stopped again.

CHAPTER 39

CHRIS NOTIFIED US when he was ready to start the autopsy in case we wanted to observe. The others told him no thanks, but I went and recorded the findings.

"Like I said at the dump site, she is malnourished and dehydrated, she has multiple stab wounds, rodent bites, and of course the hole drilled into her forearm. She also has burn marks on her feet." He paused to stare at the lifeless mess, and it made me wonder how he coped with his job. He literally stared death in the face every day.

"Do you have the cause of death?" I inquired impatiently.

"Yes, and it's not pleasant. She died from drowning in her vomit, which was nothing but stomach juice and a small amount of water. I assume it was her body's reaction to the hole being drilled into her arm. She probably went into shock first, and since her mouth was covered—"

I filled in the blanks for myself, so I held my hand up to stop him. I couldn't bear to hear the words. The mental image was more than enough. Actually, it was too much.

"I found something different on her than the others besides the obvious hole. I found burns on her neck that are consistent with a taser," he informed me.

I paced the floor in the cold room while rubbing my arms to warm them up. "So, chloroform wasn't his go-to kidnapping aid with her. I wonder why. Did something prevent it, or is he just changing up his methodology?" I was speaking to myself, but he shrugged in response. "Was there anything in her toxicology report?"

"No. She had no drugs in her system," he quickly replied. "The only trace was metallic shavings in the wound on her forearm, which just confirms that a drill was used."

I grunted in frustration. "What is the time of death?"

"Well, she wasn't as cold as the others, so she wasn't refrigerated as long. She could have been killed as late as yesterday," he replied somberly.

I cracked my knuckles and mentally scolded myself for doing so. "That gave him nine days to torture her," I calculated. "Good God. I can't even imagine."

He nodded while stitching the corpse back up. "I bet most prisoners of war are treated better," he mumbled.

I shook my head in disgust and took a copy of his report back upstairs to inform the others. I found them huddled together by Eric's desk.

"What's going on?" I inquired.

Liam looked up from the computer monitor and told me, "There's been a mass murder in a parking garage near the Arch, and it appears to be gang-related."

I was stunned, and it took a long moment to find my voice. "How many fatalities are there?"

He rubbed his hands together and frowned. "Six fatalities. Four tourists were shot and killed, while two were repeatedly stabbed."

I felt sick to my stomach, and my palms began to sweat. There were roughly between eighty to one hundred gangs in St. Louis, but one came to mind—the Bloods. Maria said they were going to do something to flush me out. Taking me to a crime scene was a good way to do that, except for the fact that I wouldn't be alone. Although, they wouldn't be alone either, and I had no idea how many members ran with each pack. They constantly grew in numbers only to shrink after territory wars.

"Do we have any witnesses?" I squawked.

"Not yet we don't," he said with a scowl. "Of course, if there are any, they might be afraid to come forward."

I bit my bottom lip. "Mounted cops are usually patrolling the area, so that might be why they chose a parking garage. Didn't the attendant know anything?"

He shook his head and looked back at Eric's computer. I nudged in to get a better look at what they were doing. They were going over surveillance footage from the security cameras in the garage. After another minute, the carnage blurred by, so Eric backed it up several frames.

Eric froze the first frame and pointed to the top right of the screen. "They approached the victims from this direction at 10:07 according to the time stamp."

We watched in horror as five gang members took out a crowd of people coming off the elevator on the third level of the parking garage. The chaos was gut-wrenching as bodies crumpled to the ground in a large pile of death and decay, and we all gasped. The video footage was in black and white, so we couldn't see the gang's colors, but I didn't need to. I recognized two of the gang members as Bloods from my days in the Drug Unit.

"They're Bloods members," I announced. "They are a part of the Tenth Street crew"—I pointed to the frozen frame on the screen—"I recognize him and him."

Liam picked up Eric's desk phone while telling us, "I'm going to send SWAT in for a raid. I'll tell them to bring in as many members as they can, and we'll try to match them up to the footage. Eric, print a few of the frames out, so we have a visual." He turned toward me. "Do you have the autopsy results?"

"Yes," I answered and then rattled off Chris's findings. They wondered the same thing I did about the taser—why the change up? "It could be because he runs the risk of killing them with the chloroform, and he'd rather do it slowly through torture," I theorized.

"Or maybe he has a partner," Marisol mentioned. "We've considered it before."

I paced the area in front of my desk while I reconsidered that possibility. "In killing teams, someone is usually the dominant partner. I suppose the submissive one could be abducting the victims while the dominant one inflicts the torture, but that doesn't answer the question of why change from chloroform to a taser unless they both do abductions."

"Regardless, without any trace evidence or eyewitnesses, we don't have any suspects," Eric muttered. "So, that leaves us at ground zero."

Before we could continue the conversation, Jamie Tinsley stepped into the office. "What's up, Jamie?" I asked. "Please don't tell us there's another missing person."

He looked down at his shoes before speaking. "I guess I won't be very popular today then because there is. A young man went missing from Sunset Hills, so the SHPD called us. They're worried it has to do with your open case." He handed me a piece of paper that had the man's information on it.

I read it aloud for the others. "According to his wife, Jake Bennett was headed to the shopping plaza on Watson Road to do some shopping at the Home Depot early this morning, and he never came home or called. His car is still in the parking lot, but he's nowhere around. He was paged in all the stores, and he's not answering his phone. The car has already been processed, and there are no signs of a struggle."

"Damn!" Eric yelped and slammed his fist down on his desk, causing his coffee to spill onto the floor, which he didn't seem to mind. "How do you go missing in broad daylight from a crowded plaza?"

It was a viable question. "Are the police sure he just didn't take off with someone willingly? Did they make sure there weren't marital problems that would cause him to run off?" I wondered while trying to find my answers in the report.

"Yes, all that was asked. She swears they are two peas in a pod, and he would never leave her. He was there to buy supplies for decorating the nursery; she's six months pregnant," Jamie responded.

"We need to get his photo all over the news. Someone in that parking lot or in the store had to see what happened," I declared. "He didn't just vanish into thin air." That gave me an idea. "Liam, what do you think about setting up a press conference to talk about the case? Without giving the specific details, of course, we can just brag about how we have leads we are looking into. I think that will put the heat on him and make him finally screw up."

He opened his hands in a shrug. "Run it by the captain, and if he says okay, then I think you should do it since the killer is fixated on you."

"Of course, that might put you at more risk," Marisol mentioned.

I nodded. "I know, but it goes with the job." I went to the captain's office and got his permission to proceed, so I called the KMOV station and set it up. Liam went with me, while Eric and Marisol remained at the station to work on the mass murder case involving the Bloods.

We met with Ronnie Maylor, one of the news anchors, and began the interview. She said it would air on the evening news tonight. I didn't discuss the specifics of the case, such as the killer's MO or signature, but I did allude to the fact that we had suspects in mind without specifically saying so.

I told her the killer was likely intelligent, charming, attractive, around thirty years old, organized, and well-educated. I also mentioned he was probably employed and single.

At the end of the interview, I looked into the camera and said, "This has been a traumatic time for the St. Louis area, but we have direction, and it's only a matter of time before justice is served. We encourage anyone with information that can help us with his capture to come forward."

Liam raised a brow at me when I was finished and ready to leave. "Where did all that come from?"

I smiled up at him. "FBI profiling one-o-one."

He clapped his hands together. "All right then. Let's hope it works and pisses him off enough to start slipping up."

CHAPTER 40

HE WENT TO the basement to check on the curator and his new arrival, who spent several hours out of it from the scopolamine injection. It had been too difficult to stand him up against the wall because the drug made his legs like rubber, so he chained him to a table instead. He was okay with that because it was new to him. It kept the thrill for him fresh.

He visited the curator first and offered her a drink of water. Then he picked up the leather flogger he'd purchased at an adult store in town and fondled it while she watched with gaping eyes. His dream about the detective had given him the idea, and he was anxious to try it out. He taped her mouth up first because he had a headache and didn't want to hear her screams. She shook her head rapidly though.

"Oh don't worry. It only stings a little bit. A lot of people actually enjoy using the toy," he told her in a soft voice. "I've never tried it myself, but there's no time like the present."

He approached her, running the leather fingers through his hand, and reared his arm back. He struck her across her hip a few times and then stopped because it wasn't doing anything for him. He needed to see and smell blood.

He picked up his knife and carved a vertical slash into her exposed right forearm. The blood trickled down in a crimson stream, and he caught it in the water bottle.

"There's no need for concern. I'm not a vampire; I'm not going to drink it," he assured her. "And while I'm not going to live forever, I'm certainly going to outlive you."

He approached her with slow steps to watch her fear escalate, occasionally taking a photograph. Then he dragged the knife tip across her abdomen, relishing how her face contorted from the pain.

"Now it's his turn," he sneered and pointed toward the table with the knife. "What do you think I should do to him?"

She squeezed her eyes shut in response. He knew whatever it was, she didn't want to see it because she was intelligent enough to know it could happen to her too. He approached the man, who was looking all around his confines, and smiled at him.

"Welcome to my humble abode. I'm sorry that your five-star suite was downgraded to this, but I'll try to make your stay as uncomfortable as possible." He held up the knife and watched the gagged man's face blanch. "Don't worry. I'm not going to stab you, at least not yet." He set the knife down and picked up his hammer, which came crashing down on the man's face just hard enough to shatter his nose.

The redhead screamed into the tape and thrashed his body against his chains, but they were firmly bolted to the table. He had no chance of escape.

He stared down at the man writhing in agony and wondered how long it took him to realize he was going to die. *What is it like to know death is coming for you?* Sadly, he, himself, knew exactly what it was like.

CHAPTER 41

BY THE TIME we got back to SLCPD, SWAT had several members of the Bloods brought in, so we met up with Eric and Marisol to view the lineup. I identified the two I'd crossed paths with before, and we picked out the other three involved in the mass killing from the remaining eight in the lineup. The five were sent to booking and then put in interrogation rooms.

I was in the room with Terrance Johnston, whom they called T-bone. "So, Terrance, what was this about?"

He tried to play it cool by shrugging my question off. "Bitch, I don't know what yo' talking about."

I narrowed my eyes at him. "Terrance, we have you on video surveillance. You and your buddies are going away for this for a long time—life probably. But I'm willing to tell the court you cooperated if you give me some answers."

He waved me off. "Bitch, yo' sure be tripping. I ain't saying shit," he spat.

I grabbed my things and stood up. "That's okay, Mr. Johnston. I'm sure you'll enjoy prison, but I hear the

Aryan Brotherhood is strong where you'll be going. Do write me and tell me all about it." I walked to the door.

"Wait! I'll talk," he said and stopped me.

I smiled to myself before turning around. "All right. I'm listening."

He confessed to being there and to killing one of the victims. He said they were there because the new leader in Carlos Garcia's place, Darnell Robins, sent them. He wouldn't say why, but I knew it had to do with me.

After all the interviews were completed, we had five confessions. One of the men, Quintrell Harvey, gave us the reason. He said Darnell had sent them and told them to hide inside or behind cars until I showed up to investigate and then take me out.

I told Quintrell, "Well, if you hear from him while you're in custody, you can tell him I said nice try."

It was finally time to go home, and I was beat.

I fixed chili for dinner and turned on the news while I ate. I hoped the killer was watching the evening edition to see my interview, which I made sure ran on several stations.

Duke begged for some of my supper, but I denied him. If I wanted someone next to me who was farting all night, I'd get married.

Just as I was starting the dishes, my interview came on. *Yikes! The camera does add ten pounds.* My phone rang about half-way through it, and it was my mother.

"I'm fine," I answered and then listened to her ramble on for ten minutes about how I probably wasn't fine at all. "Mom, you can't worry about every case I have. I've been a cop for seven years now," I reminded her.

"I know, and your father and I have worried about you every second since you started," Karen Delossa scolded me.

I rolled my eyes. I loved that they cared, but it wasn't ever going to change my mind about my career. Not even this case was going to do that. I promised her I was keeping an eye on Denise and that I was being careful. Then we said goodbye. A minute later, Justin called.

With a groan, I took the call. "Hello, Justin."

"Hey. I heard you brought in the perps responsible for the mass shooting in the parking garage this morning. I guess my calendar is going to be full for a while."

"You're welcome," I teased. "I know how you like to stay busy."

He laughed and asked, "Is your sister staying with you tonight again?"

"No, I think she's working tonight."

"Oh, that's right. You said she works at that gas station on Grand," he uttered.

"Yep. She's one of the shift managers," I affirmed. "It's just to help put her through college. I did tell you she wants to be a prosecutor, didn't I?"

"Yeah, I think you mentioned it once. I'll help her if she has any questions." I heard his microwave beep in the background.

"I'll let her know. Enjoy your supper," I told him.

"How did you know I was heating up something to eat?" he wondered.

I chuckled, "Because I'm a detective. It's what I do."

"All right, Super Sleuth. I'll let you go, but if you get lonely, I'm a phone call away," he flirted.

"Good night, Justin," I said firmly and hung up.

Before the sun went down, I took Duke for a walk. This time, though, I was sure to take my Glock, Mace, and taser. Aside from the highway noise, the muggy evening was nice and quiet. There was a rain breeze kicking up, so I didn't go too far before turning back. I knew how Duke felt about the thunder, and it looked like there was going to be a violent storm.

Just as soon as we started back, the rain began to fall with thunder rumbling in the distance. I picked up my pace to a light jog to get there sooner, but Duke pulled hard on the leash, forcing me to run.

I dried him off when we got back and then took a hot shower before bed. For the first time since I became a homicide detective, I had nice dreams.

CHAPTER 42

HE STILL HAD room to fill. He needed another soul to put in his collection, so he drove around St. Louis, hunting for prey. He didn't have anything particular in mind. He didn't like to discriminate when choosing his victims. However, he never chose children or elderly individuals. He needed healthy men and women who could withstand the pain for his purposes.

He saw her—a mousy woman standing at the bus stop all alone. She was digging in her purse, probably looking for enough change to pay the fare. He pulled up to the curb and rolled down the passenger window.

"Excuse me, but I'm lost. Can you give me directions?" He held up a street map for emphasis.

The woman looked around anxiously but then approached the Suburban. "What are you trying to find?" she asked.

"I'm trying to find Jones Street. I was told it was by Tenth Street, but I can't find it on the map."

The woman scratched her head and mumbled, "I've never heard of Jones Street, but I know where Tenth is."

She opened the door to look at his map under the dome light. The light that caught her eye, though, was the electric light of the taser as it zapped her hand. Her body violently convulsed, and he pulled her into the SUV before anyone could see. Then he put zip ties on her hands and ankles and quickly drove to the vacant house. He had considered selling the house and just using the smaller one, but he liked the larger studio it sported. He also didn't mind the drive between the two. When his mother had finally left his bastard of a father, she tried to get as far away from him as she could afford.

Since the drive to Town and Country would take a while, he injected his new guest with scopolamine. She was a lightweight, so he hoped he didn't use too much of the drug on her. He wanted her completely lucid for what he was going to do, so he would wait until the effects wore off.

She was still out of it when he carried her into the house, so he chained her upright in a chair. It would do until he could move her to the wall. He didn't bother to photograph her because there was no pain or sorrow. He went upstairs to paint while flipping through his collection to find the perfect inspiration.

He settled on a couple photos of the curator. He liked looking at the broken-down mess she'd become. He worked the canvas with shades of grey and black before accenting it with the blood-red paint mix. He laughed at the irony of painting her portrait with her own blood. He'd be sure to show it to her when it was completed. He would show it to the whole world when he was finished. Of course, no one but him would know who the subject was. It wasn't like the detailed portrait of the lovely detective; it was simply a portrait of pain. He added some more shadows, and it was done.

He stepped back to admire his work with a smile. In the morning, he'd take his paintings back to the City Museum and talk to the new curator. If he was still rejected, he'd take them to another museum. Unfortunately, though, only the City Museum had the art show for new artists this holiday weekend which was coming up.

He readied himself for bed and quickly fell asleep. He dreamed he achieved the fame he sought…before it was too late.

CHAPTER 43

July 1, 2016

FRIDAY WAS MY father's birthday, so I called him when I got up for work. He was an early riser, so I knew he'd be up.

"Your mother wants you and Denise to come over for dinner and cake tonight," he told me, and his tone warned me not to say no.

"Sure. I can make it by 6:00 if that's okay," I replied.

"That's fine, and you can bring your new friend if you want. Denise told us all about him."

"Sure. Your new grandson would love to meet you. Will Buster be okay with him, though?" I was referring to their beagle, who was twelve years old.

"Shit, he's too old to fuss about another dog in the house," he answered.

"Okay. Well, I have to get ready for work, so happy birthday, and I'll see you for dinner. Bye."

"Bye. Try not to get killed today," he teased. That was always what he said ever since I joined the force.

I showered and dressed before fixing a bowl of cereal for breakfast. I made sure to set an alarm on my phone, so I didn't forget about my dinner plans. I had no idea what kind of day it was going to be or how stressed I'd be at the end of it, so better safe than sorry. I needed to buy a gift yet, so I thought about my options. I had no idea what he wanted or needed, so I decided to stop by the Apple store and get him a gift card since he was into electronic gadgets.

While most people would be enjoying a long holiday weekend, I'd be on call the entire time, and with the rapid abduction and killing rate of the St. Louis Slasher, I was sure to be busy.

I left the house twenty minutes earlier than usual in case traffic was a bitch, and it was. People were already heading out of town for the weekend. Large vehicles were towing boats as far as I could see down the stretch of highway. I walked into Homicide five minutes before my scheduled time.

"Crazy traffic this morning, isn't it?" Liam asked, looking up from the file he was reading with a secretive grin.

"You bet. I'm glad I left early," I answered and plopped down in my seat. "What's the smile for?"

"Well, I have good news and bad news. I'll give you the bad news first. A woman was abducted from a bus stop along Third Street last night. The good news is, we have an eyewitness. She'll be in shortly to tell us what happened."

"That's great!" I yelped. "That is to say, it's great if it's related to our case."

He nodded. "That's true, but she did see a flash that might have been from a taser, so I'm hopeful."

Eric and Marisol popped around the corner, and he filled them in. We all sat around, anxiously waiting for her to show up and give us direction. At 9:13, she finally appeared, and we ushered her into the conference room. She quickly explained that she was coming out of a bar along Third Street when she saw a flash of light and then a woman being pulled inside a large SUV around 10:00 p.m.

"Do you have any idea what kind of SUV it was?" I probed, feeling antsy.

"I want to say a Suburban. My sister has one, and it looked like hers, but the street lamp was out, so I could be wrong. It was dark in color with tinted windows. That's all I know."

"Did you see any of the license plate?" Marisol questioned, and she shook her head.

"Sorry, it drove off too quickly. It was all a blur once he had her inside," she answered.

"You said once *he* had her inside. Are you sure it was a man, and did you get a good look at him?" I asked next.

She looked down at her hands, and her face fell. "I was half in the bag, so I didn't get a *good* look, but there was enough light from his dome light to know it was a guy, and he's white."

Liam stood up and told her, "Thank you. This information will hopefully help us in our case. If you recall anything else, please get in touch. Any little detail might help, so don't brush it off." She agreed and then left us alone to talk in private.

Chris slapped his hand on the table. "Well, that's better than nothing," he declared. "It gives us some kind of direction."

Marisol sighed and stood up to pace the room. "Yeah, but there has to be hundreds of dark Suburbans in the area."

"Yes, but how many will have tinted windows? It's hardly standard on vehicles," I offered. "And if it's a super dark tint, there has to be a form filed with the DMV for a medical exemption."

Liam snapped his fingers. "That's where we'll start then. Look up medical exemptions on SUVs in St. Louis county, and try to limit it to Suburban models if you can."

"I have an idea. We can check surveillance cameras for nearby businesses in that area to see if they picked anything up. Possibly a bank ATM got a snapshot for instance," I suggested.

"Good idea. Let's run with it," Liam commanded. "Eric, you can look up the vehicles with tinting, and the ladies and I can go to the businesses to see what cameras have a view of the street. Also, we can check traffic cams. They might have a clear shot of the license plate. There couldn't have been that many Suburbans in the area at 10:00."

Feeling like we were finally getting somewhere, we separated to carry out our assignments. Liam, Marisol, and I found the bus stop at the intersection of Third and Biddle Streets where the abduction took place. We found the bar the woman had mentioned and walked along the sidewalk, trying to spot surveillance equipment. There was a pawn shop that looked promising, so we stepped inside and spoke to the manager.

"I have a camera on the door, and it can see some of the street," he informed us. "You can have the disc to review if you want."

We accepted the DVD disc and thanked him for his time. There weren't any other businesses with cameras pointed toward the street, so our best bet for a clear shot at the plate was the traffic cam at the intersection. I called up to the station and had someone in the department review the footage from around 10:00 last night. I told them specifically what to look for, and they returned my call when we were back at the station.

"I can see the Suburban, which appears black in color, but it has something over the license plate that is blurring the image," Officer Marsha Miller explained. "I can't make any of it out, even after applying photo enhancing techniques."

"Thank you, officer. I appreciate it," I replied with a heavy heart and hung up to explain to the others. "He used some kind of cover or spray on the license plate to cause the image to blur. I've seen such spray sold online before. The gloss reflects the flash back toward the camera, blurring the image. It's not high-tech, but it works against the traffic cams."

"Apparently, it works against us too," Eric added in a tense voice.

"Eric, did you find a list of Suburbans with tinting and a medical exemption?" Liam questioned and poised his pen over his tablet to take notes.

Eric shook his head with a loud sigh. "I didn't find anything other than one that belongs to a middle-aged couple with five kids. The husband has glaucoma, thus the special tinting."

We didn't have to say it aloud. We all knew that man isn't our killer. Our killer isn't a family man. He doesn't form loving bonds with others.

"What if he's not from St. Louis County? We should search other nearby counties for exemptions," I proposed. "It's possible he lives a considerable distance away from the crimes as a way to dissociate from them."

Liam's face scrunched up. "I suppose that's possible."

"I think *anything* is possible at this point," I pressed. "I wonder if he saw my interview on the news. He might try to change up his routine just to throw us off."

Marisol tilted her head and cocked a brow at me. "But that would make him unorganized, and the profile you gave is of an organized killer, which I agree with."

I had a gut feeling, and it was difficult to explain. "I just think he's going to do whatever he can to outsmart us. It's essential to his ego. He is playing a game, and he has to win."

Liam stood and scooted his chair in. "Then it's time we capture his pawn. Check with other counties if that's what you feel we should do. I'm going to go update the captain."

We went to our desks and printed out county maps. Then we split them up and began calling the DMV in each. The thing nagging me in the back of my mind was he could illegally have tinted windows too. He was breaking the big laws, so why not?

I called Maria and told her to keep a lookout and write down the plate number if she saw anything. She, in turn, told me to keep a lookout because the Bloods weren't done yet. With the holiday coming up and all the people that would be enjoying the outdoor festivities, I was worried to the core.

By the time 5:00 rolled around, we didn't have any workable leads on the Suburban, but, on a good note, we didn't have any more dead bodies either. At least we were done with our work on the mass murder case. It was open and shut as far as we were concerned. We had the killers and their confessions, so it was a slam dunk for the district attorney. It freed up our time to focus on this madman while keeping an eye on the Bloods.

I was exhausted when I made it to my dad's birthday supper with Duke in tow. I picked up a gift card to the Apple store on my way home from work. I figured he was due for a new phone.

They all questioned me about the case, but I didn't have much I could share with them. "All I can tell you is, he doesn't have a type, so watch yourselves. He isn't discriminating. We think he's driving a Suburban. That's about it. We don't have much to go on yet," I told them.

"Okay, now what about you and the ADA? Denise said he was there the other night, so are you getting back together?" my mother asked.

I glared at my little sister. "Denise has a big mouth, and no, we aren't getting back together. We're just friends, and he was over because I was freaked out about the case."

After I helped her with the dinner dishes, while Denise and my dad played with Duke, we all sat down for cake and a game of pinochle. Then I had to say goodnight. I was having a hard time keeping my eyes open.

I invited Denise to stay with me since Marcus wasn't back from his trip yet, and after a scolding from our mother, she agreed. On the way home, we had an incident that neither of us would ever forget.

We were stopped at a red light on North Twentieth Street and Dr. Martin Luther King Drive when a white SUV full of thugs came at us. I recognized their colors—they were, of course, Bloods. *I'm too tired for this bullshit.*

They jumped out of the vehicle, and I grabbed my Glock and taser, but I tossed the Mace to Denise. "Keep the doors locked and call nine-one-one!" I barked at her.

I exited the car, with Duke on my heels, and trained my gun on the hoodlum in the forefront. "Stop where you are!"

"Whoa, mamacita. There's no need to go all Rambo on us. We just want to say hey to you and your girl," he drawled with a slur. "Plus, it looks like you're outnumbered."

Duke let out a low, vicious growl to let them know I had plenty of backup.

"You boys took a wrong turn," I threatened with a snarl. "I suggest you get out of here right now."

Out of the corner of my eye, I saw the leader's homie reaching for his gun, so I shot the taser, bringing him down to the ground in a shuddering heap. One of the others thought he'd catch me off guard, too, but he was also wrong. I shot him in the kneecap with my Glock when he drew his weapon, and he crumpled in a groaning pile on top of the other. Duke tackled the third man to pull a gun and clamped down on his throat. That just left the big talker and one more. Sirens closing in made those two run for the SUV.

"This ain't over, bitch! We've got your number," the pack leader yelled over his shoulder while I cuffed his buddies. Luckily, I had zip ties on me at all times. They were easier to carry than metal cuffs, and I could carry several.

"And my dog has yours," I hollered back with amusement.

"Ouch! You shot my fucking knee," the one yelped while I yanked him to his feet.

"Yes, and I'll shoot the other one if you don't shut up!" I growled, kicking their guns toward my car.

Three patrol cars showed up and called for an ambulance while giving me a questioning glance. They knew me, but I flashed my badge for any onlookers.

"You kneecapped him?" one of the young officers asked with a grin.

I shrugged. "He drew first."

"Okay. I get that. Can you call your dog off this one, though?" he asked, pointing to the perp in Duke's snarling grasp.

I whistled for my new partner, and they took the scum away. I told them I'd fill out paperwork on the incident in the morning. I was too tired to do it tonight.

"That's fine. These asshats aren't going anywhere but lockup tonight," the senior officer told me.

When Duke and I climbed back inside my car, Denise gaped at me. "That was like...wow. I didn't know you could be such a badass," she stated in awe. "I knew Duke could, but not you. Respect."

I laughed, "Do you feel safer staying at my place then?"

"Oh hells yeah," she replied.

We drove to my house, and I went straight to bed. I sure had an interesting story for the watercooler tomorrow.

CHAPTER 44

HE TOOK HIS art collection back to the City Museum and met with the acting curator, Randy Michaels, after work. The man seemed snooty at first, but then he warmed up and practically drooled all over the paintings.

"I think these will make a fine addition to the art show," he raved. "For a new artist, you have plenty of talent with room to grow. Are you attending school?"

"No," he grunted. "I'm teaching myself, but I have had classes in the past."

Mr. Michaels looked at the paintings again. "Well, raw talent should always be honed into fine skills, by whatever means you choose, but these will certainly do for now." He squinted his eyes. "That's a lovely shade of red; it's kind of crimson but not quite."

He smiled and wondered what the man would do if only he knew the truth. "It's a special blend I made by mixing a few mediums."

"It works. I like the way it pops in contrast to everything else. Let me print out an agreement between you and the museum for us to display your artwork in the gala this holiday weekend. We shall split the sales seventy-thirty. It's a great way to get discovered and to be permanently featured in the museum." He was already busy typing something into his laptop. "Now, spell your name exactly how you want it to appear."

"My first name is S-E-A-N, and my last name is spelled P-E-I-R-I-C-K," he told the curator.

"Terrific. Now, you'll want to be here for the gala to network with the other artists and the buyers of course. It starts at 9:00 tomorrow and runs until we close at 7:00. We are closed Sunday and Monday for the holiday. Anything that isn't sold can be claimed by you to take home, or you can leave it with me to consider it for placement among our collections. If I don't place it, I'll return it to you." He held out some papers. "Please sign these if you agree."

He signed his pen name with a steady hand. He had no doubts about anything the curator said. He was certain his work would be sold or placed. They shook hands, and he accepted a copy of the signed documents. His paintings remained there, so the staff could set them up with the others on display for tomorrow's gala.

When he left the museum, he picked up takeout for dinner and went to the house in Town and Country to check up on the mousy woman. According to her license, her name was Margie Moore, which perfectly suited her librarian appearance.

"You know, taking the bus can be very dangerous," he taunted her as he approached with his butcher knife. "And didn't your mother tell you not to talk to strangers? Mine did, but strangers weren't the ones I needed to fear. However, I won't bore you with the details of my abusive childhood that probably turned me into the stand-up man I am today. No, I believe in showing rather than telling."

He used the tip of the knife to cut off the top buttons of her blouse. It was just enough to expose the tops of her small breasts.

"Please," she begged. "Please don't do this. You don't want to do this."

He tilted his head and grinned. "Oh, but I do. You see, I don't want to die alone."

He raked the knife across her collarbone, spilling her essence into her B-cups. He picked up the empty canister he had nearby and collected enough of it to mix up another batch of blood-red paint. Then, because his head was still pounding, he covered her mouth with duct tape, stifling her screams.

"Sorry, love, but I've got a headache from hell. You understand, don't you?" He tapped her on the chin in an almost sweet gesture. "I'll check on you in the morning. Sleep well."

He left her chained to the chair because he didn't have the strength to struggle with chaining her to the wall. He stopped walking up the stairs and turned back to look at her and the vacant wall chains, forming a brilliant idea. He decided to leave her there and take on another guest, and he knew just whom he wanted. He wanted the detective's fine-looking sister. He'd done his homework, so he knew where she lived and where she worked. Taking her would definitely lure Sasha Delossa to him. He laughed to himself. *I've never done sisters before.*

CHAPTER 45

I WOKE UP early Saturday morning and took Duke for a run while Denise slept in. I had my Glock on me, but no one was causing trouble in the neighborhood. I'd have to go into the station later to fill out the paperwork for last night, and I was going to take Denise with me since she was my eyewitness. I figured it couldn't hurt to have her backup my story for the defense attorneys.

When I got home, Denise had breakfast on the stove, so I took my shower. Then, after we ate, we went to give our statements because she had to work later. It didn't take long to provide our testimonials and sign the necessary forms.

"It looks like a pretty cut and dry case, but you never know what the defense attorney is going to say about it," Officer Davis told me. "He might say you fired your weapon unnecessarily, and then there's the dog to consider."

I smiled and replied, "Well, I'm sure ADA Sinclair will get this case, and he knows me. It will all be fine. Also, there's a traffic cam at that intersection, so pull the footage. They ran a red light to cut us off."

"Will do," Officer Davis replied. "If there's anything, I'll find it and let you know."

I waved my hand at him. "Just let me know if there's a problem; otherwise, you don't have to worry about it. I don't expect there to be any issues."

"Fair enough. Enjoy your day," he chirped and waved goodbye as we left. I could tell he was checking out my sister, so I teased her about it on the way to her place.

"Can I borrow Duke until Marcus gets back?" she asked and batted her lashes.

I laughed, "That doesn't work on me, darling sister. However, you can come over tonight if you want. Here's a key for you and my alarm code." I handed her a spare key and a piece of paper with my security code written on it.

"Uh-oh…I see a dognapping in the near future," she teased.

I reached to the back seat and petted Duke. "He'd never leave me willingly. He loves me too much."

"Well, I'll just have to keep coming over for my visitation rights then," she giggled as she climbed out of my car. "Thanks for the ride home. See you later."

I waited until she was safely inside before I pulled away from the curb and headed back home, making sure no one was following me. Justin called as soon as I walked through the door.

"I heard you were involved in a brawl of sorts last night, and now I have to work over the weekend. I really should spank you," he razzed me.

I laughed at the image. "Well, I had to work, so why not you? Besides, they started it." I made myself sound like a rebellious teenager.

"Hmm…well, you'll just have to make this up to me then. How about having dinner with me one night this week? I'll even cook," he suggested.

I looked at my wall calendar and saw that I didn't have anything going on. "If I have to make it up to you, why would *you* do the cooking?"

"I want to show off my skills. Besides, you'd be making it up to me just by being here," he responded.

"And is that all?" I questioned.

"Well, you can help me with dessert." His voice was full of innuendo, and I felt my cheeks flush.

"Oh, I don't know about that. I think we should behave and stay friends," I sighed.

"We could be friends with benefits then," he purred suggestively.

I rolled my eyes. "So, strings attached? Is that what you're suggesting?"

He laughed, "No, not strings, benefits. I'm your friend regardless, but why not have some fun with it? Not to mention it's a form of exercise."

The fact that he was trying to talk me into bed was borderline hysterical, and I had to fight to hold back my giggles. He sounded so much like a lawyer with his closing arguments.

"Counselor, I'll have to get back to you on that," I teased.

"Okay, okay. I'll change the subject. What are you wearing?" he joked.

"Oh, I'm wearing a skimpy pair of shorts and a filmy tank top," I lied. "And while it's hot outside, I think I could still cut glass."

He blew out a deep sigh into the phone. "You're just being mean. Want to do something tonight? No strings attached."

I considered his proposal, but I wasn't up for company. "I think I just want to be alone. If I change my mind, though, I'll call you."

"Okay. Talk to you later then. Bye." He quickly hung up, but I heard the disappointment in his tone.

I just can't be whom you need me to be. I'm too tangled up inside, especially now.

I cleaned up the breakfast dishes and made my grocery list out. It was time for this little piggy to go to the market.

CHAPTER 46

HE ANXIOUSLY PACED the gallery as several pairs of scrutinizing eyes looked over his work, assessing every minute detail. Buyers knew what they wanted to purchase when they walked through the door, and if they didn't see some semblance of it in a piece, they quickly moved on. His work was no exception to the rule, and he felt his temper rise each time someone turned their nose up at his art. One bitch had commented to her escort that he hadn't "used enough color," while another said they "didn't make sense." If he had the time, he'd follow those cows out to their cars later and teach them a thing or two. Instead, though, he chose to develop thicker skin.

A pretty brunette stared at his portrait of the curator. "I love this piece," she exclaimed. "I can feel how sad the subject is. It's so real." She was talking to the middle-aged woman next to her, but he was the one who bothered to reply.

"Thank you. I appreciate the compliment," he gushed, causing her to spin around.

"Oh my goodness! Are you the artist?" she inquired with a big smile.

"Yes, I'm Sean Peirick. Thank you for admiring my work." He reached out and shook her hand.

"I was just thinking about how real it feels. How do you capture so much emotion?" Her curiosity was endearing.

"I study people and their expressions, habits, and what have you," he explained. "It helps me to capture the human psyche."

She looked back up at the painting. "Well, you're doing a good job of it." Her eyes fell to the price tag, which read one-hundred-fifty dollars. "I want it for my collection. Will you sign the back?"

He nodded with a large grin. "I'd be honored to."

She waved over one of the museum employees to take it down for her. "I want this one," she announced and pointed to the painting.

"You have an excellent eye for art, ma'am," the employee mumbled and handed her the piece. "You can pay over there." He pointed toward the exit where staff members were taking payments and security was standing guard.

He knew the compliment about her eye for art was said at every sale because he'd already heard it numerous times regarding other artists. However, in this case, it was true. He accepted the piece from her and scrawled his autograph on the back with the pen she handed him.

She looked at it with a smile and exuberantly told him, "Thank you! This is so great, and I have the perfect spot for it in my living room."

"You're most welcome. Please check out my other pieces while you're here," he replied and pointed to his other works.

"I certainly will," she chirped and wandered off to examine them just as another group of people came through the door. Things were looking up for him.

By the end of the art show, he'd sold four of his seven pieces and made five hundred-fifty dollars. He'd hoped, of course, to sell them all, but he was pleased nonetheless. He left the remaining three pieces at the museum for consideration. Just as he was preparing to leave, Randy Michaels stopped him.

"Mr. Peirick, you've had a wonderful first show. I hope you aren't disheartened that everything didn't sell," the man said.

"I'm not. I'm rather pleased with how it turned out, and I hope you'll find a permanent home for the three remaining pieces," he replied.

Mr. Michaels shifted his weight from one leg to the other. "I'm not the only one who decides, so I can't guarantee anything. I'm rooting for you, though."

He shook the man's hand. "I'm glad. I'll be on my way then, and I look forward to hearing from you." He needed to get out of there. He had hunting to do.

CHAPTER 47

HE WATCHED HER through the convenient store's windows while she worked, and the pretty young woman had no idea. She was too busy bantering with the customers and the other employee to notice him.

When the young man carried the trash out to the dumpster, he made his first move. He used enough chloroform to be lethal this time. Just to be sure, though, he also stabbed the lad ten times. Yes, it was overkill. No, he didn't care.

He waited until the customers were gone, and the pretty manager went looking for the young man. She followed the lad's path out to the dumpster and shrieked in horror. She quickly turned to bolt inside, but he blocked the entrance. There was a jolt of electricity before she could scream again, and she crumpled to the ground in a quiet heap. He picked her up and carried her to the Suburban, tucking her away in the backseat after giving her a shot of scopolamine. He bound her hands with bondage cuffs and put tape over her mouth, so she'd be ready for the first wave when they reached Town and Country.

He carried her into the house and down the steps to the basement where Margie looked up in surprise.

"You've got company Minnie Mouse," he told the frightened woman while propping the unconscious victim up against the wall. "You'll welcome her, won't you?" He kept the body propped while attaching the cuffs to the hook in the wall above her head. Then he used smelling salt on her to let the games begin.

Her eyes fluttered open, and panic widened them. She tried to talk, tried to scream, but only muffled sounds came out. She looked all around, noticing Margie chained to the chair, and tears began to roll. She knew exactly who he was, and she knew her fate, or at least what the evening news was willing and able to report. Even her sister, the tough cop, couldn't save her now. No, this was one time she'd lose.

"Welcome," he purred with a malicious grin. "I'm guessing you didn't expect your evening to turn out this way. I'm sorry to ruin your plans, but that's what they say about life, right? 'Life happens when you're busy making other plans.' I'm sure you have an idea about the kind of fun you and I are going to have, but if not, let me show you."

He deftly wielded the knife and slashed Margie across her cheek. Then he turned to Denise and growled, "Your turn."

She shook her head violently, but he looked at her with pure contempt in his eyes. There was nothing but evil in his stare. There was a dark chasm of malevolence and death where a soul should be. Then there was a flash of steel as the knife came down on her.

CHAPTER 48

MY CELL PHONE woke me up from a sound sleep just after midnight. It was SLCPD calling, and my heart leaped into my throat. *He's killed again.*

"Hello?" I answered with a yawn.

"Sasha, this is Liam. I need you to come in right away," he said with urgency.

"Has he killed again?" I asked even though I knew he had.

"I'll give you the details when you get here. Everybody has been called and is on the way. See you soon." The line went silent, and I jumped out of bed, wondering why he didn't answer my question.

I quickly put on my clothes and gear and ran through the living room. I glanced at the sofa to tell Denise I was going in, but she wasn't there. I figured she decided to go home after her shift, or it hadn't ended yet.

Twenty-seven minutes later, I stepped off the elevator and into the office. Everyone else was already there, and they all looked up at me with grave expressions.

"What's going on?" I inquired with a shaky voice. No matter what I could imagine, their faces told me what had happened was worse.

"There's been another murder," Liam stated and gestured to the lit-up map. "A customer at the Shell station on North Tucker said no one was attending the register or working in the store, which was being looted, so he walked around the building to the dumpster area and found a young man stabbed to death. He immediately called nine-one-one and hid until the police arrived. They recovered the body, which Chris is examining now, and found a name tag on the ground next to the body. It doesn't belong to the young man, Sasha. It belongs to—"

"Denise Delossa," I yelped before he could say it. Then I fell to my knees with tears flooding my eyes. "She had to work tonight. Oh God!"

I felt someone's hand on my back as I completely unhinged. I'm her big sister and a cop. I should have been able to protect her from this horrid nightmare.

"It was him, wasn't it? It was the Slasher, and he has her somewhere," I sobbed. I knew I needed to call my parents, but I wanted to wait until we had all the facts. "What do we know for sure?"

"Until Chris tells us otherwise, we just know that the man was repeatedly stabbed, and they smelled something sweet on him," Liam answered.

"Chloroform," I theorized and ran to the stairs with them following me. I took them two at a time and burst through the doors to the morgue. "Chris, tell me what you know."

"He was dosed with a lethal amount of chloroform and already dead when the killer stabbed him ten times. The difference in the wounds is that a pocket knife was used. The Slasher has been using a butcher knife," he explained. "I'd wonder if it was a different perp, but there's no trace in this case either. We didn't recover prints, fibers,

DNA, or hairs on the body. I doubt two killers are going to be that cautious, especially in a violent crime like this," he answered.

"What about security tapes? Did you bring those in?" I asked impatiently.

"Yes, everything we could recover was brought to the crime lab. I'm just waiting for someone to bring me the reports," he replied.

Just then, the door to the lab opened, and a tech I didn't recognize handed him a file folder. I stared with a thudding heart while he read over the report.

"There is footage of the murder and of a young woman being abducted. She was tased and then dragged away. I hate to say this, but you can't see the killer's face in any of the footage. He had a hat pulled down to hide his face," he told us.

Again, I felt a comforting hand on my back, but it didn't provide any relief. I had anger, grief, fear, and a desire for revenge jumbling together to burn hot in my throat until it made me vomit in the sink.

After I rinsed my mouth out, I turned to the others and told them, "Taking my sister wasn't random. He knows she's my flesh and flood. This is just another way to target me."

"But how would he know she's your sister, and why is he targeting you? Why not one of us instead?" Eric wondered aloud.

I shook my head and threw a hand up in the air. "The hell if I know. Maybe he has something to do with one of my old cases. I don't think a gang banger would be this organized, but who the hell knows? Why didn't he take the man instead? It has to be because of me."

"Well, we don't take a look at any other cases until this one is solved," Liam declared.

"I want to see the video footage," I blurted and started toward the crime lab.

"Are you sure you want to? We'll take a look at it," Eric said, following me.

"I have to see it. It might be the last image of my sister alive," I sobbed.

I hated to say the words, but they were true. I hated that I would have to give my parents the notification of her death. First, though, I had to notify them of her abduction. I looked at my watch; it was 1:30. It could wait until a reasonable hour because there was nothing they could do. Someone in our family should be able to get sleep tonight. There was no reason we all had to suffer every minute of it. I'd call them before the morning news, though. They couldn't hear it like that.

"Please replay the surveillance footage for us," I asked the lab tech, and she quickly obliged. Liam and Marisol had joined us, so we crowded in to view the recording. "Pure overkill," I mumbled while we watched the dead young man get repeatedly stabbed with gloved hands. Then my sister came on the screen, and the room began to spin for me. "Oh God," I cried out as I watched her body violently spasm from the electrical current. Then he just dragged her across the ground like a ragdoll until they couldn't be seen anymore.

"Chris was right. We can't see his face with his hat pulled down like that," Eric grunted in frustration.

I stared at the dark, faceless image. "Where are we at with getting the rosters for James Sutton's classes?"

"To be honest, I don't know. It fell by the wayside with everything going on, but we certainly need to find out," Liam responded.

"I think we need to compare the art classes to forensics classes and see if anyone is taking both. He knows how to clean up after himself. He knows how to hide in plain sight," I told them.

"We aren't going to be able to get that information until Tuesday, so we need to find a different direction. We need to follow up on those two houses where no one was home," Eric mentioned. "There was the one in Eureka and the one in Parkdale."

"I'll call the police departments today," I offered. "They can go check them out even though it's a holiday weekend."

"If they won't, we will," Liam affirmed. "We'll also call the FBI today. There's nothing else we can do at this hour, though, so maybe you should try to get some rest."

I shook my head. "No way. The dog is fed and can let himself out. I'm not leaving. I can't sleep knowing what he's doing to her."

"Speaking of dogs, do you have something of hers the police dogs can sniff? We can take them around locally and to the houses we need to revisit," Eric suggested.

I rubbed the back of my neck while trying to think. "Yes, she spent the other night on my sofa. I'll bring in the sheet and pillowcase." I looked up at Liam. "We should also have them sniff the belongings of our missing persons. We know he has them locked away somewhere too."

"Agreed," he replied.

We went back upstairs to strategize for the day, and then I fell asleep at my desk until my alarm woke me at 5:00. I had to see my parents and tell them the horrific news.

CHAPTER 49

HE GOT UP early because he was too excited to sleep. He immediately went downstairs to visit his newest guest. Her head snapped up, and she shook it while trying to yell something through the thick tape.

He wagged a finger at her. "Ah-ah-ah. You need to save your energy, my pet," he chastised. "Trust me that you'll need it for what's in store for you."

He turned toward Margie and pulled the tape back to give her some of a meal replacement shake. He only let her have half, though, before putting the tape back in place.

"You have to share with your companion," he sniped. He turned to Denise Delossa and smiled. "If you start complaining or yelling, I'll take the supplement away, and you'll starve. Think about that," he warned. He pulled just the corner of the tape back and stuck the straw in her quiet mouth. She finished off the drink, and he replaced the tape. "That's my good girl. This is all I had to eat most of the time when I was a kid. The only time I had a decent meal was at school. Do you know how hard that is on a growing boy?" Both ladies shook their head to appease him. "Of course you don't because you were busy leading your perfect lives," he spat and withdrew his switchblade.

He approached Margie first. Her eyes went wide with terror, and he lifted the camera strung around his neck to snap a photo. Then he plunged the knife into her left forearm and took another. After he withdrew the weapon from her bloody flesh, he turned it toward Denise.

"Denise, Denise, my pretty pet. How long I've wanted to do this to your sister, but I guess you'll have to suffice for now," he threatened. The scared woman shut her eyes tight, though, depriving him of his photo opportunity. "No! Open your eyes. I need to see your pain," he commanded, but she kept them closed. He reached out and touched her cheek, causing her to flinch. "Of course, I could just cut your eyelids off or prop them open with toothpicks, but I didn't want to be that cruel. I'll leave it up to you."

She opened her eyes, and he took her photo. She looked perfectly confused and utterly terrified, especially when he raised the knife again. He lifted her shirt just enough to expose her stomach, and he sliced the knife across it, causing copious amounts of blood to spill.

"Oops! I think I cut too deep, and I can't have you dying on me just yet," he chuckled and reached for something on the table behind him. It was a needle and thread. "Sorry, but I don't have any lidocaine. At least, I don't have any that I care to share," he sneered and began to stitch her up while humming to himself. Her wincing and tears only added to his pleasure. It almost made him forget the jackhammers pounding in his head. His cell phone inside his pocket rang. He held a finger up and told them, "Excuse me, ladies, but I really need to take this call."

"Hello?" he answered and then was silent to listen to the caller. "Oh my God! That's just awful. I'm so sorry, and I'll be right there. Bye." He hung up and focused his attention on Denise. "Sorry, my pet, but I must go. Your big sister *really* needs me."

CHAPTER 50

AFTER I LEFT my parents' house, I went home to collapse for an hour before I went back to work. Instead of sleeping, though, I called Justin and explained what had happened. He promised to come right over. I had to be strong in front of my parents and my co-workers, but for now, I just needed to be vulnerable with someone. For now, I didn't have to pretend to be a hero who would save the day in the end—I surely didn't feel like one. I collapsed on my bed with the dog and bawled my eyes out. Sensing my pain, he whined and tried to lick my face to cheer me up.

Justin knocked on the door thirty minutes after we hung up. I had to deactivate the alarm to let him in, and then I had to hold Duke back from knocking him over.

"Whoa! Call off your bodyguard," he teased and ruffled Duke's fur.

Justin sat on the sofa and patted the cushion for me to sit next to him. Before I could, though, Duke got in the way and sniffed him from head to toe, whimpering.

"Have you been petting other dogs?" I joked. "He did the same thing to me when I got home from my parents' house this mor—" My voice choked off in sobs.

Justin stood up and led my quivering body to the couch, forcing me to sit down. He put his arm around me and squeezed.

"I'm so sorry this is happening to you, babe. What can I do to help?" he asked.

I looked up through my tear-filled eyes and growled, "You send him straight to the chair without delay when we catch him. That is if I even bother to bring him in alive."

He rubbed my arm and made a shushing sound. "You're going to catch him before it's too late. She'll be fine."

"How can you say that?" I squealed. "Even if he doesn't hurt her, and of course he will, she'll never be the same after suffering his abuse and torment." I pounded my fist on his chest. "He'll probably torture her more and kill her faster than the others because of me!" I jumped up and grabbed my purse. "I have to get out of here. I have to go back to the station."

"You need to rest," he pleaded with me. "You're no good to yourself or your team when you're sleep deprived."

"I'll sleep when I get my sister back alive and well. Get out!" I yelped, and Duke, sensing my tension, growled at him.

He jumped up and stepped around the angry animal. "Okay, I'm leaving." I followed right behind him, and so did Duke.

I knelt down and hugged my gentle giant. "Go back inside, sweet boy. I'll be back later." I pointed to the door, and he dutifully trotted back in. I set the alarm and raced back to SLCPD.

Everyone was still there, and it made me so touched, I started crying again. "I can't believe you all stayed."

Eric patted my back. "When something affects one of us personally, it affects all of us personally. This team is here for you."

"I'll second that," Marisol agreed.

Liam stepped out of Captain Roman's office and gave us the news. "We'll have everything we need to solve this case and get the other victims home. The FBI is on its way to assist."

"What about those two homes that need searching?" I wondered. "Has anyone been in touch with the Eureka PD?"

"Yes," Liam answered, "the one in town belongs to an elderly couple, and it's a recreational room in the basement. The home in Parkdale is up for sale, so they dismissed it, thinking the home obviously couldn't be shown to prospective buyers with bodies in the basement."

I countered, "Unless he's using that as a ploy to lure new victims. I wouldn't dismiss it just yet. We should check into the listing to see whom it's through and when it was listed."

Liam gave in, considering my circumstances. "All right, if you and Marisol want to check on that, Eric and I will check elsewhere. However, let's wait a little bit for the FBI to get here, so they can help."

"I have the address written down in my notes, so I'm going to start calling realtors while we wait on the feds. Too much time has already passed," I explained and brought up realty agencies serving the Eureka area on my computer. There were several to contact, so we split the list up.

No one showed that property as a listing, though, which made it all the more suspicious.

"I looked it up in the database we all use, and it's not in there. There wouldn't be a sign in the yard unless the house was listed in this database," an agency supervisor explained to me just as the federal agents walked in.

"Okay, thank you for the information. We'll take it from here," I told the woman and excused myself off the line.

"What did you find out? You look like you have bad news for us," Eric claimed.

I tilted my hand back and forth. "It depends on how you look at it. The house isn't in the real estate database, thus indicating it isn't really listed. So…" I stood up, ready to bolt out the door.

Liam grabbed his gun and badge. "We're on our way now! Agents, we'll fill you in during the drive."

Agent Gould went with Marisol and me, while Agent Pullum went with the men, and a K-9 unit with three police dogs followed us. We were armed. We were ready. The tension in the air was palpable, and my heart raced like a cheetah on fire. I silently prayed and told my sister I was on the way.

We pulled into the driveway, spreading the vehicles out to hinder any chance of escape. The dogs had smelled items from all the victims who were still missing and were chomping at the bit to start their search. So was I.

The house and property were eerily quiet. The nearest neighbors had to be at least a mile away, making it the perfect spot to hide the most heinous activities. We knocked on the door while the K-9 officer searched the perimeter with the dogs.

Intense barking pierced the still air as the dogs pawed at the basement windows. "Here!" the officer yelled out, and we rammed the front door down without blinking.

Our team and the FBI agents ran down the stairs with our guns poised while the K-9 officer and dogs searched the main floor for our perp. My heart stopped when we saw the horror beneath the floorboards. A man was chained to a table, sporting multiple gashes and an obviously shattered nose. A woman was chained to the wall with equally excruciating wounds. Both had their mouths covered with duct tape, but their eyes spoke their thoughts in volumes. *Thank you for coming to save us!* We used bolt cutters to break them free and called for two ambulances and local law enforcement.

"Who did this to you?" we demanded in unison. "And where is he now?"

Jake Bennett told us he was just helping the guy with car trouble, confirming it was a black Suburban with tinted windows.

"I-I-I know who he is. His name is Sean Peirick. He's an artist and wanted his work to be displayed in the City Museum," Tiffany Clark bawled. "I denied him, though, so he did this. I don't know where he goes when he's not here." Her voice trembled along with her body, so her words were broken up with violent shudders.

The K-9 officer and dogs came running down the stairs. "He's not here," Officer Ryan announced. "There's an art studio upstairs and a cot but not much else."

I looked down at the three overly-excited dogs and told them, "Good job, officers."

Sirens filled the air along with red and blue lights as the Calvary came. I promised the victims they would be okay, and while I certainly hoped that to be true, I couldn't help but wonder if Denise was. Neither had seen her, and only Tiffany Clark had seen one other victim—the late Tamara Boyd.

After the ambulances were taking off toward the hospital, I turned to Chief Thomas and said, "The name she gave me is Sean Peirick. Do you know him?"

She shook her head. "No, but we'll be getting to know him really soon. That's a promise. My men searched the house, and there's no mail or anything with a name on it. We'll have to check the property records and see what we come up with. Did you get a physical description for him?"

With a disgusted sigh, I told her what I knew. "They both claim he's tall, thin, and has brown hair, but he always wore a hat pulled down low. Even when he went to the museum with his artwork, she could barely make out his face."

"Just like on the video," Eric chimed in. "Hiding in plain sight."

"Let's get a sketch artist in to see her nonetheless," I suggested. "If he wears the hat everywhere, maybe she can remember what it had on it, and hopefully, someone will recognize it."

We gathered our things up and went back to the station to figure out the rest of the puzzle. Chief Thomas promised to find out about Sean Peirick and to get the sketch to us as soon as possible. Once we had it, it would be publicized all over the news. We already had a tip line set up with operators manning it twenty-four hours, and Liam said we would add more phones and staff once the sketch was released.

We left, but several local officers stayed behind to man the house in case the killer returned. I just couldn't think where else he could have taken Denise and Margie Moore. Where were they being held and tortured? I hoped my sister could withstand it. Finding Jake Bennett and Tiffany Clark alive made me feel optimistic.

CHAPTER 51

JUSTIN KNEW WHAT was going on in the Parkdale house. He had a camera app on his phone to spy on his guests. The police were very smart to come back to the house and find his two visitors, but they would never find the house in Town and Country. If his father hadn't, how could they? His mother had taught him the art of hiding. Sure, it had been a little too late considering all he'd endured growing up, but it was useful to him now. She'd put the house under a new identity—Madeline Hughes—so his father could never find them. When she passed away several years ago, Justin left it that way, even after finding out his father had died in a drunk driving accident. He left the Parkdale house in his father's name, Robert Marx, which couldn't be tied to him either since he'd changed his last name to Sinclair when he was eighteen and then hidden all the records when he became a lawyer. It was a benefit of working in the judicial system.

It's like I was never even there.

Of course, the Town and Country house wasn't where he lived either. He had a condo in Webster Groves.

He paid the property taxes and utilities for the two homes out of his parent's estates, so nothing was traced back to him. He didn't want the world to know the stock he'd come from.

While on the way to Town and Country, he called Sasha. "Hi. I just wanted to check up on you. How are things progressing?" he asked with deep concern.

"Well, believe it or not, we found two of the victims and sent them to St. Clare Hospital. It looks like they're going to make it, but there was no sign of Denise or the other victim, Margie Moore. We are all headed back to SLCPD to figure out the next step," she replied. "Luckily, the FBI came back to lend a hand."

"That's great that you saved two people from him," he raved. "And that probably means Denise is still alive too, so don't lose hope." *Actually, you probably should be losing hope right about now because I don't know that she's going to stay alive.*

"I'm trying to stay positive. Do me a favor, will you? I need an arrest warrant for a Sean Peirick. Can you get that pushed through for me?"

He smiled smugly to himself. "Sure, I'll do that for you once I get back to the office. I'm on the road right now. I have to go to a deposition."

"Get it as soon as you can, please. I need to go, but I'll be in touch. Bye." She hung up, and he laughed hysterically.

"Sure, and while I'm at it, I'll get one for Santa Claus and the Easter Bunny too. Your chances of finding them are just as good," he mused aloud.

Instead of heading to Town and Country, he made a turn and headed toward St. Clare Hospital in Fenton. He needed to check on his witnesses. Even though he always wore a hat of some kind when he was breaking the law, he couldn't risk them giving a positive I.D. Also, he wanted to finish what he'd started.

CHAPTER 52

JUSTIN TOLD THE nurse at the nurse's station that he was a sketch artist there to talk to Tiffany Clark and Jake Bennett. Since security would be tight, he'd glued on a false mustache and used a black temporary color spray for his hair. He was no amateur.

"She's down the hall in the last room on the left. An officer is watching over her, but he must be in the bathroom," the nurse stated, and he followed her gaze to the vacant doorway. He was lucky the real sketch artist hadn't shown up yet.

"Thank you," he replied with a smile and shuffled down the hallway with his sketchpad and pencil in hand. What he had in his pocket, however, was another story. He rapped on her doorframe and announced, "Hello? I'm Officer Baker here to sketch your description of the man who abducted you."

His outfit fooled her, and she welcomed him in. Her eyes scanned the door for her watchdog, though. "Where is Officer Kramer?"

Justin looked over his shoulder. "He said he needed to relieve himself. Don't worry. You're in good hands." He sat in the chair next to her hospital bed. Luckily for him, her I.V. was on that side. "Go ahead and describe everything you can recall about the man," he encouraged, and his left hand quickly put the details to paper, while his right hand concealed a syringe full of potent ketamine.

When she closed her eyes to search her memory about the details she could recall, which was mostly about the hat he'd worn, he injected the drug into her I.V. It took three seconds for her to go into cardiac arrest, and the alarms on the monitor began to blare. He jumped up to get help just as Officer Kramer ran through the doorway.

"What happened?" he demanded.

Justin shrugged and looked back over his shoulder. "I'm not sure. I was sketching her eyewitness account, and then her eyes rolled back, and the alarms went off."

Nurses and doctors ran into the room with a crash cart, so he and the officer both dove out of the way. The paddles were used on her, and epinephrine was injected into her heart, but it was too late. She was gone.

Officer Kramer shook his head solemnly. "Did you at least get enough information?" he asked while glancing at the incomplete drawing.

Justin looked down too. "Not really. She went into cardiac arrest right after we started. I guess the stress of reliving the ordeal was too much for her."

A passing nurse overheard him and reported, "I think it was the malnutrition. It weakened her heart."

"How horrible," he mumbled and left the room to find Jake Bennett.

When he got to Mr. Bennett's room, the man was sitting up in bed and holding a pregnant woman's hand. *Damn!*

Justin made eye contact with the officer standing guard and mumbled, "He needs his loved ones now, so I'll come back in twenty minutes. If you'd just let him know, I'd appreciate it."

"Sure," the man grunted and looked down the hallway in both directions. He took his job seriously, but little did he know...

Justin wasn't worried about the man's account. He'd had the hat on, and then the man's eyes were swollen shut for the most part after Justin had broken his nose. His biggest threat was out of the way.

Whistling, he went to the parking garage and jumped into his Jeep. The Suburban was resting in the garage at the house in Town and Country. He put on his ultra-dark sunglasses as a pounding headache came on. Doctors had assured him they couldn't do anything to remove the large tumor, and it was only a matter of months before he died.

But you first. He headed toward Town and Country. He needed a word with Denise.

CHAPTER 53

JUST AS WE got back to SLCPD, I received a call from a nurse at St. Clare Hospital. She called to inform me that Tiffany Clark had died of a massive coronary.

"Between the malnutrition and the torture, her body just couldn't handle the stress," the nurse told me.

"That's awful," I cried. "Do you by chance know if the sketch artist met with her first?"

"Actually, there were two here. I sent one to her room right before she passed away, and the other came later after she was gone."

My skin crawled at the implication. "I need to know what they looked like. How were they dressed, and did you see a name tag on them?"

"Well, the first man was in a white shirt with dark slacks, but he didn't wear a name tag. He was tall, thin, had black hair and a mustache. The second man was in a police uniform, and his name was Officer Meyers if I remember correctly," she explained.

The victims hadn't said anything about the killer having a mustache, so I deduced it was a disguise. They'd also said his hair was brown, not black. Someone was going through a lot of trouble to stay hidden.

"If Officer Meyers is still there, please provide him with the details of the first man and fax it to me at 800-555-2227. It's very important that you do so. I have reason to believe he is the killer we are hunting, so if you see him again, alert security immediately," I calmly advised her.

She gasped, "Oh my Lord! I will certainly do that. I had no idea."

"I know you didn't. Hiding is what he does best," I assured her. "Please tell Jake Bennett's officer to be extra vigilant."

"I'll go talk to him right now, and I'll get the sketch to you as soon as I can. I can always call the station and have them send another artist if the one isn't still here with Mr. Bennett."

I thanked her, ended the call, and relayed the disturbing conversation to the others, who were trying to dig up information on Sean Peirick. They were unable to, though, even with the FBI's resources. He was one step ahead of us yet again.

An hour later, the drawing of the fictitious sketch artist came over the fax machine, and we immediately released it to the public via the news stations. We did add a notation that the man in the drawing was probably wearing a disguise.

"We believe he is actually clean shaven and has brown hair, but he was seen with black hair and a mustache today. He often wears a hat to conceal his face, and he is using the assumed name Sean Peirick," I told them, and they aired the captured photo from the Shell station security camera. "Anyone with any information is urged to immediately call the tip line. To our knowledge, he has two people in his custody, and we need your help to bring them safely home to their families." I didn't mention that my sister was one of his prisoners because that would just put her in more danger.

Shortly after the broadcast, an interesting call came through the tip line. A woman claimed she'd just purchased a painting from Sean Peirick yesterday at an art gala.

"He even autographed the back for me," she said in a shaky voice. "The gala was at the City Museum. I'll bring it in if you want me to."

"If you would bring it to the station, it just might help," I told her. "Also, please provide our sketch artist with an accurate description of how he appeared at the time."

CHAPTER 54

HE'D HEARD THE broadcast over the radio in the Jeep just as he reached his mother's house. Nothing tied the name Sean Peirick to him, except for the check from the museum that he would shred, so he wasn't worried about a paper trail. He'd worn a large mole on his cheek yesterday for the museum gala, and he'd used a red rinse in his brown hair.

"You just keep chasing your tails," he laughed to himself. "You'll never figure me out."

His hand flew to his head; it felt like it was in a vice grip. He didn't keep any prescription medications at this location, so he went to the bathroom and popped three aspirin. When he went home later, he'd put on a new fentanyl patch.

After washing the color out of his hair and the mustache glue off his face, he took a meal replacement shake to the basement for the women to share. "If you scream when I uncover your mouth, I'll plunge this knife into your chest, and then you can bleed out for the rats," he threatened. "Do you understand?" They both nodded weakly, so he fed them the shake. Then he focused his attention on Denise. "Your sister is becoming a pain in my ass," he seethed. "I really thought we could get back together, but now I'm not so sure." As if she didn't already know who he was, he took off the hat to let it really sink in. "I had to comfort her earlier because of you, and I think if you were found dead, she'd completely turn to me for solace."

Denise squeezed her eyes shut to block him out, but he wasn't going to let her off that easy. He pressed a finger along the stitches in her abdomen until her eyes flew back open.

"I want you to look at me," he spat. "I want you to see what is coming for you."

He turned to Margie and brandished the knife, which then came down on her left hand, removing the pinky finger. Her face turned ghostly white while her eyes nearly bulged out of their sockets. Her screams were muffled by the tape, but he heard enough of her pain and terror to give him an adrenaline rush. He took some photos to use later.

"Now, it's your turn, my pet," he threatened Denise. He cocked his head at her when she seemed almost accepting of whatever torture he was about to inflict. That bothered him. "Aren't you afraid? You should be," he chastised. "Did your sister teach you to always be brave?"

He grabbed a handful of her blond hair and lopped it off with the knife. Then he grazed her neck with the tip of the blade, spilling just enough of her crimson nectar to satisfy him. He matted the hair with the blood.

"I'm going to send SLCPD a care package," he claimed with maniacal laughter. "I'll see you girls later, and lucky for you, I'm going to be around more often."

He went upstairs and found a baggie to store the finger and hair. Then he headed to his home in Webster Groves, where he put the items in a bubble mailer. Wearing gloves the whole time, he addressed the package to Sasha at the police station. He recalled that he was supposed to get her an arrest warrant for Sean Peirick, so he needed to come up with an excuse for not having one. He sent her a quick text.

I don't want to bother you while you're working, but if you want that arrest warrant, I'm going to need the man's address.

He figured either she'd tell him the address in Parkdale, or she'd tell him there was no such person in the area. He medicated himself and sat on the sofa to wait for her response. His legal secretary already knew he'd be out the rest of the day, so time was on his side. He was drifting off to sleep when his phone chimed.

The address is 201 Morgan Ridge Drive, Parkdale, 63049. However, I don't think it's in his name.

He got on his laptop and printed out a fake warrant. Then he took his package to the FedEx box in town, so she'd get it tomorrow.

CHAPTER 55

LUCY SANDERS SHOWED up at the station with her painting by Sean Peirick forty minutes after we ended our call.

"Sorry it took a while to get here, but I live across the river in Cahokia," she explained. "Anyway, here it is."

She held up a black and white silhouette painting of a woman with red tears, which was presumably bloody tears. That reminded me of the red painting of me, and I called down to the crime lab.

"I need a swab done on another painting, please," I told Jackie, and she immediately came upstairs.

"Do you think this is blood again?" she voiced, and I nodded.

"I just wonder whom it belongs to," I declared. "Also, why did he paint it?" I turned to Eric, who was studying the piece. "While I talk to Miss Sanders, could you see about getting a psychologist in here? Perhaps the police shrink will come in."

"Sure," he replied and went to his Rolodex while I invited Lucy to sit by my desk. "So, I'll call up the sketch artist in a minute, but I have some questions first. Did you talk much with him before purchasing his artwork?"

She looked down nervously at her lap. "Not really. I was talking about how much I liked the piece, and he told me it was his work. That's when I asked for his autograph, and that's pretty much the extent of the conversation."

"Did you recognize him from the area?" I asked.

She shook her head. "No. I always go to the galas for new artists, and I've never seen him or his work before."

"Hmm…I guess he's new to art then, or he's just new to this community," I stipulated and ran another search in NCIC, using some of his newer parameters. I looked up crimes with lacerations, broken bones, and burns, but nothing came up with a combination of the factors. I also looked up holes that were drilled into the body, and it was also null.

"You're just a different kind of evil, aren't you?" I mumbled to myself.

"Did you ask me something?" Lucy questioned, and I felt my face redden.

"No, I was just thinking aloud. I'm going to get the sketch artist up here." I made a call down to the main floor and was told someone would be up shortly.

The first person to step off the elevator, though, was Jackie, and she looked excited. "The red substance was blood mixed with paint again, and the DNA matched your recently deceased victim, Tiffany Clark," she informed us.

Lucy jumped up from her seat. "Ew! I bought artwork with someone's blood on it? Who is this creep?" she shrieked loudly.

"He's a serial killer and at the moment, impossible to catch," I mumbled under my breath. "As unfortunate as your situation is with the painting, you're quite lucky you didn't get hurt or murdered by him."

She put one hand to her mouth and the other to her heart. "I was talking to the St. Louis Slasher? I don't believe it," she whispered and slowly sank back into the chair.

"Yes, you were, and I'm glad you're all right. We'll need to keep the painting until after the case is over," I informed her.

She waved a hand at me. "Keep it forever. I don't ever want to see it again."

Jackie was still standing there, and she cleared her throat. "There's one more thing about the blood. We have a hair this time, and it has the root bulb attached. It's in analysis still, but I'll bring up the results as soon as I have them."

I clapped my hands together once. "That's terrific news! Maybe we can finally nail this son-of-a-bitch."

The sketch artist, who freelanced with the station, showed up and led Lucy to the interview room for quiet and privacy. The man in the final drawing had a mole on his right cheek and reddish-brown hair. We thanked Lucy for her cooperation, and she quickly left since her part was finished. Again, she told us to keep the painting.

I held up the sketch of the Slasher and studied it along with my partners. "So, you fancy yourself a master of disguise, don't you? Well, I'm a master at puzzles," I murmured aloud. "Eric, did you get ahold of the psychologist?"

"Yes, but she can't make it until tomorrow morning. They're doing their holiday celebrating with family today," he replied.

"Okay. I'll be here bright and early," I told them, and then I went down to the crime lab to wait for the results on the hair follicle, hoping that we were finally getting somewhere.

CHAPTER 56

July 4, 2016

I WOKE UP at 4:00 Monday morning and took Duke for a jog. I had my Glock strapped on for security, but my own safety wasn't on my mind—Denise's was.

Last night, Justin had come back over and held me while I cried. He'd tried to put the moves on me, but I brushed him off. I needed comforting, not sex. I didn't let him spend the night, either, because I didn't want him to try again.

He'd given me an arrest warrant for Sean Peirick, but the man was still a fart in a hurricane. We had no record of him anywhere. The house in Parkdale had once belonged to Robert Marx, but he had died in a drunk driving accident in 2001. He had a son, David Justin Marx, but we had no idea where he was. The house was current on property taxes, with the money coming out of Robert Marx's estate, so the government never batted an eye. I had to wonder if the son was our killer, and if he didn't go back to the Parkdale house, where would he hide out?

Hopefully, the hair follicle would give us some answers. I also held hope that the psychologist would give us some understanding of the killer's psyche. If we could figure out his next move, maybe we could prevent it. My gut wrenched when I considered that it might be to kill my sister, and I said another prayer for her.

By 7:45, I was at my desk at SLCPD, going over the hair follicle reports again. The DNA wasn't in CODIS, but we were able to identify that the hair was brown, and reports showed the donor was on fentanyl, Decadron, and phenytoin. The fentanyl was for pain and stronger than morphine, the Decadron was a form of chemotherapy, and phenytoin was for seizures. Jackie had told me the combination of drugs pointed to treatment for cancer.

By 8:00, the others had arrived, and so had a psychologist named Dr. Fitzgerald, who was there to look at the paintings of Tiffany Clark and me. We studied her face while she looked over both pieces.

"This red one conveys a lot of anger. Red is a power color that demands attention to be paid. It's like he is saying *look at me*," she told us, and I couldn't help but think his crimes said the same thing. "This other one is showing a lot of pain and grief. One would think the artist is suffering from something."

I looked at my team and commented, "That goes with the theory that he probably has cancer. Maybe he wants the attention because he is dying."

"One can only hope he's dying," Eric sniped, and I mentally agreed, but I didn't want to display hostility in front of the psychologist.

"If the artist is dying, I don't anticipate him stopping until he dies," Dr. Fitzgerald added. "It's likely his killings will just grow more frequent and intense as his suffering becomes worse because he doesn't want to suffer and die alone. He feels like he is alone in the world."

I shook her hand. "Thank you, Dr. Fitzgerald. Your insight helps us to understand the motive better."

Liam spoke up before she could leave. "Why is he mixing blood in with the red paint? He used blood from five victims in the red piece and one victim in the other."

She appeared shocked by the news and looked at the pieces again. "It could be just another cry for attention, or it could be because he wants you to know what he's done, so you can catch him. As he nears the end of his life, he wants the recognition he deserves. He wants the credit for the killings, and he wants people to remember him always."

"So, it's possible the torture will get more dramatic then, so he can outshine other serial killers?" I wondered.

"Yes, absolutely. He wants to be exceptional and remembered for what he brings to the table," she answered. "He wants to be differentiated from all others."

"He wants his own signature," Marisol summed up.

Dr. Fitzgerald looked at her watch. "I've got an appointment to get to, but please call if there is anything else I can help with. I've always been fascinated with forensic psychology, and I'd actually like to interview the suspect when you capture him."

I nodded. "That shouldn't be a problem. We'll be in touch."

After she left, Liam mumbled to us, "It looks like the worst is yet to come then as he deteriorates."

A tear ran down my cheek. "And it will somehow involve my sister." I wiped away the moisture, not wanting to come apart at the seams in front of my team.

"I wish we could cross-reference the list of medications with patients to narrow our search down," Eric said, and I had to agree with him. It would certainly make things handier.

"At least he finally got sloppy. Hopefully, he'll do something to totally give himself away soon," I remarked. "Then again, if he does, it will probably be because he's reached the end, and he might choose to go out fighting."

Eric rapped his knuckles on his desk. "I think you're right."

"We should be able to get a warrant for patient records at the local cancer centers," Marisol announced. "Then we can narrow the pool down to match our profile." She jotted the thought down on her notepad.

"That's a great idea, but since it's a holiday, we aren't going to get it done today," Liam replied and put his head in his hands. "I feel helpless as we wait for him to make the next move. I'm tired of him calling the shots."

My desk phone rang and made us all jump. "This is Detective Delossa," I answered.

"Happy Fourth of July, detective," a creepy voice greeted me. It was the same voice as before, and it was just as full of taunts as the last time. "Are you getting closer to figuring everything out?"

I mouthed, "It's him," to the others. Then I turned my attention back to the Slasher while pressing the speaker button on the phone. I needed to keep him on the line long enough for Eric to run a trap and trace.

"I think we are. How much time do you have left? How long have the doctors given you?" I asked him.

There was a long pause before he answered me. "What makes you think I'm ill?" His voice had irritation in it, and I knew I'd caught him by surprise.

"You got sloppy," I taunted. "We know you have cancer, but you can't use that as an excuse to hurt others."

There was another pause. "You don't want to piss me off when I have your pretty little sister in hand, do you?"

I bit my lip and took a risk. "Please let her go and take me instead. If you want someone to be there at the end of your life, I'll be there for you. I won't let you die alone."

He laughed, and it sounded full of evil. "Oh, I won't be alone, and I assure you that we'll be meeting soon," he threatened and then hung up.

We all looked to Eric for information. "Did you get anything?" I squawked.

He shook his head in disgust. "No. The call was coming from a disposable phone, and it bounced off three towers. He knows what he's doing."

I wanted to rip my hair out. "I can't handle this. Did I just get my sister killed?" I yelped.

"I don't think so. Whatever his end game is, I think he wants you to see her again," Liam speculated.

"Great," I huffed. "So, he'll want me to watch her die then."

A loud rap on the doorframe got our attention as a FedEx driver stepped into the office. "I have a package for Detective Delossa," he announced and looked around at our confused faces. "We don't normally work on holidays, but the sender used FedEx Custom Critical for it to be delivered here today."

I raised my hand, and dread filled me. "That's me."

"Sign here, please." He thrust the electronic device toward me and then handed me a large envelope, which I quickly opened to reveal a bubble mailer with blood stains on the outside.

"Oh God!" I cried out when I saw the contents, and I quickly dropped the package. The finger peeked out and made the other detectives cringe too. Luckily, the driver had already left.

"Get that to the lab," Liam said to Eric, and he quickly scooped it up and headed for the stairs.

"Was the finger the only thing in there?" Marisol asked.

I shook my head with tears streaming down my cheeks. "No. There was a lock of bloody blond hair too. My sister is a blond."

I had been a cop for several years, but this was the worst moment of my career. I felt helpless, useless, and enraged. I felt torn apart. I covered my mouth with both hands and screamed as loud and hard as I could into them until my throat and lungs burned. I saw concern in my co-worker's eyes, but I could tell they were right there with me.

Jackie rounded the corner from the lab twenty minutes later and gave us the results. "The finger's DNA doesn't match the hair, but the hair and blood on it are from"—she looked at me as her voice softened—"your sister."

"Was the fingerprint in IAFIS?" Eric asked, and she shook her head. "Then it must be from the missing woman, Margie Moore. Unless he's taken another victim."

"But where is he keeping them? We raided his house," I yelped. "If that *was* his house."

Liam ordered us all to go home and get some rest until something else came in on the case or until tomorrow, whichever came first. I didn't want to go home just yet, though, so I found myself driving to Webster Groves to see Justin. I needed a shoulder again, and I couldn't face my parents without rays of hope to offer them.

CHAPTER 57

HE DROVE AROUND the city, hunting for his next victim. Lightning bolts of pain stabbed his brain, and he wanted to take it out on someone. He shouldn't have to suffer alone. He wasn't in the mood to torture or abduct, just kill, and it didn't take long for him to set his sights on the one he wanted—the middle-aged man looked a lot like his father.

There was no ruse to lure the man to his death. He simply exited the Suburban with a wooden baseball bat and bludgeoned the man in a vacant alley. The man, who was evidently homeless, pleaded for his life and safety, but it fell on deaf ears. Every time he felt a stabbing pain in his head, the bat came crashing down on the man, even long after he was clearly dead. The man's skull was turned to mush as was his body. Blood squirted out of every orifice under the weight of the bat, painting the pavement hot red. With each deathly blow, he pictured his father's face, even when he could no longer recognize the man's. Every strike was a bloody home run.

When he was out of breath, he drove back to Webster Groves like he'd never been there. He put on clean clothes and a new fentanyl patch for the pain. Then he called the doctor's office to complain about recurrent nausea. The nurse promised him that Zofran would be called into the pharmacy by the end of the day.

He was ready to lie down for a quick nap when there was a soft knock on his door. He looked through the peephole and saw Sasha. Her nose and eyes were red from crying, and he could see her body trembling.

CHAPTER 58

I KNOCKED ON Justin's door and waited patiently for him to answer. When he did, I told him that I needed comforting after a difficult morning.

His face fell. "I had hoped my visit last night soothed you a little."

"I appreciated your company, but it doesn't take away my panic for my sister," I replied with a glare.

He put his arm around me and led me to the sofa. "I know it doesn't, hon. I just hope it helped some."

I sank into the soft sofa cushion and leaned against him when he sat beside me. "It did for the moment, but now I'm in hell again. He sent us a grisly package today. Correction. He sent *me* a package today."

"A package? Like another painting?" he inquired, and I shook my head while covering my eyes.

"No, it was much worse. It was a pinky finger and a bloody lock of my sister's hair," I revealed with a shudder.

"Oh my God! He cut of Denise's finger?" he yelped and pulled me tighter against his frame.

"No, it was someone else's finger. We think it belonged to Margie Moore, but for all we know, it could be someone else. We only know it belongs to a woman," I explained. "The psychologist who looked at the artwork says he's demanding attention because he's sick. We know, based on medications found in a strand of his hair, that he is being treated for cancer. We think he's killing people because he doesn't want to suffer and die alone."

He rubbed my arm, trying to soothe me, but it wasn't working. Actually, it was irritating me, so I pulled away and stood up to pace the room. I felt a tension headache coming on.

"I'm scared out of my wits, Justin. I'm scared he's going to kill her or scar her for the remainder of her life," I wailed. "I don't know how to catch him."

He got up and walked toward the kitchen. "I'm getting a drink. Do you want a glass of water or tea?"

"Yes, some water," I answered and headed to his bathroom.

While I was in there, I opened the medicine cabinet to find some aspirin. I got more than I bargained for, though. I saw prescription bottles lined up, so I snooped. He was on fentanyl patches, Decadron, and phenytoin. He was on the killer's medications, and his face slammed into my mind. Only it was wearing a mole and reddish-brown hair. Then it was wearing a mustache and black hair. I could see it now. He was tall, and thin, and he was our killer. The St. Louis Slasher was trying to comfort me while holding my sister captive and torturing her. I reached for my Glock, but then I let go. I couldn't bring him in without definitive proof, and I needed Denise's location, too. I grabbed a piece of toilet paper and pulled hairs out of his comb and razor, wrapping them up in the tissue, which I then shoved into my pocket. I needed his DNA, and I needed a way out of his condo without creating suspicion.

When I emerged, I rubbed my eyes, making sure I had his attention. Then I forced a weak smile. "I'm so stressed out, I won't make good company right now. I'm going to go home and rest. Maybe I'll come back later, though," I told him and accepted the bottled water he'd brought me. "You owe me dinner after all." It was so hard to play nice with him, but I had no choice. I couldn't blow my cover.

He reached out to touch my cheek, and I had to fight the urge to cringe and jerk away from him. "Yes, I do owe you a home-cooked meal. If I remember correctly, you like lasagna, so I'll use my mother's recipe and make that for you."

I rubbed my stomach. "Sounds good, and it will be the first real food I've had since Denise was taken." I let my voice soften and dropped my eyes to the floor. "I just can't take not knowing what he's doing to her, but I don't want to know either. Does that make sense?"

He nodded and squeezed my shoulder. "Sure, it makes sense. I don't blame you one bit."

He pulled me in for a hug, and I forced myself to endure it and even wrapped my arms around him to return the embrace. It was like trying to swallow a brick. I counted to three and pulled away.

"I'll call you when I get up from my nap," I promised.

"Okay. Drive safe and rest well," he murmured before planting a kiss on my lips.

Bile began rising up my throat, so I didn't let him linger. I turned away and slowly left. When I reached my car, I pulled onto the highway before picking up my phone and calling Liam.

"I found our killer, so assemble the masses! I'm bringing in his DNA, and I'll explain when I get there," I declared.

"I'll get everyone back in. See you soon, and excellent work!" he responded and hung up.

For the first time, I saw hope for rescuing my sister. It had to be him, because why wouldn't he have disclosed his medical issues to me if it wasn't? I turned on my red light and raced back.

We stood in the lab, anxiously waiting for the DNA extraction machine to spit out the comparison results. When the paper printed, Jackie analyzed it and smiled.

"It's a match," she chirped and handed the paper to Liam, who took a second glance.

Only they knew who it matched to. I didn't tell anyone else. It was too unbelievable that the ADA would be our killer. It was horrific that I'd dated him and considered him a friend.

"Let's get our warrant for his arrest," Eric hollered and banged his hands together.

"No! We have to find the location for Denise and Margie first," I hollered. "Let's search property records under his name." I turned to run up the stairs, and I heard them behind me.

We all got on our computers to search property records, but the only thing that came up was his condo. *Where the hell are you, Denise?*

"Could he have the land in another name? We know it's not under Sean Peirick, and the Parkdale house is in Robert Marx's name. Is that his father? Let's look up his birth certificate while we search for any other real estate under the name Robert Marx," Liam said.

"There's nothing else under that name," Eric announced with disappointment. "What is his mother's name?"

"I don't know his parents' names. He never talked about them," I reported. "But we learned that Robert Marx had a son named David Justin Marx, so it has to be him. Maybe it's under his mother's maiden name, but I don't know it, or maybe it's under David Justin Marx or Justin Marx."

"Those names aren't turning anything up, and I can't find Justin Sinclair's birth certificate either," Liam grunted. "It's in a sealed record, and that would take a court order to unseal it. We don't have that kind of time."

"Then we have to follow him to the location where he has Denise. I don't think he'll give it up if we arrest him now. He'll try to make a deal for the location, and by then, it might be too late to save her and Margie," I rambled. "Also, I don't want him to have any deals. I want him to *fry*," I added.

Liam nodded in my direction. "I agree, but how do we get him to go there? We could stake out his place until he's on the move, but I'd rather he go there sooner than later. It will give the women a better chance at survival since he's been starving them."

I thought about how to get him out of the house. "I told him I'd come over for dinner. I think if I call to cancel, he'll get pissed off and go to her. Let's get near his place, and then I'll make the call," I suggested, and they agreed.

"Do we want to get the FBI here first?" Marisol asked.

"I don't think we have the time for that. This is our case, and we're bringing the bastard in," Liam answered in a clipped tone, and I silently thanked him.

We rushed downstairs and rounded up the K-9 officer on duty again just in case the dogs needed to search the grounds. For all we knew, he might have cadavers buried everywhere. We sped back to Webster Groves to just outside his condo. We were in unmarked cars and hidden among other vehicles so he wouldn't see us. The K-9 unit was down the street, waiting for us to direct him. I made the call.

"Hi. I'm not home yet because I stopped by my parents' house first to talk. I don't feel up to dinner now. The day and our conversation have me too upset. Will you forgive me?" I asked and rolled my eyes. I hated playing the role of his friend. I wanted to tackle him and shove my Glock down his throat.

"That depends on you. Will you reschedule for tomorrow?" He sounded cocky, and I gritted my teeth.

"Yes, I can do that for you," I promised. "I'm sorry about tonight. I wouldn't make great company, though, so I'm saving you from a bad evening if you think about it." I was thinking about the kind of evening he *was* going to have, and I smiled to myself. He'd be spending his evening with a bunch of hoodlums in lockup. Hoodlums he helped put away.

"Okay, rest up and call me later to let me know you're doing all right," he ordered.

"I promise. Bye," I replied and hung up. Then we restlessly waited.

CHAPTER 59

LUCKILY, WE DIDN'T have to wait too long for him to leave his house. We made sure to have eyes on him as we followed at a safe distance. Liam called the K-9 officer and told him the direction to travel to catch up with us. He had to linger back, however, or he'd be spotted in the K-9 SUV. We followed Justin's orange Jeep through rush-hour traffic all the way to Town and Country.

"I don't believe it!" Liam growled. "We checked all the properties out here with outbuildings and permits."

"Go easy on yourself," I replied. "He's breaking the law, so it's quite possible he doesn't have a permit."

He shrugged. "I suppose so."

It was almost laughable to me that we were the ones hiding in plain sight now. My blood rushed through my veins as I thought about arresting him. Of course, we had to be prepared for a shoot-out too, especially since he was dying. He might try to go out via suicide by cop. I had to admit to myself that I'd rather see him rot in prison for the rest of his miserable life. He didn't deserve the easy way out.

He turned off on a back road, so we hung back for a minute, not knowing if it was a private drive or not. When we started in again, we found out that it was, and we saw his house in the distance. We also saw the black Suburban.

Liam hesitated because if Justin made it inside the house after realizing we were there, he would surely kill his prisoners. His massive ego would demand it. Once he was through the front door, though, Liam gunned the engine, spinning rocks and dirt. We kept the sirens and lights off so we could take him by surprise when we broke down the front door. I radioed the K-9 officer and told him to immediately release the dogs, so they could lead us to him and, hopefully, take him down to the ground before he could retaliate. We all, dogs included, had Kevlar vests on just in case he had a gun.

We didn't have to break the door down because it was unlocked. He was either that arrogant or lying in wait because he knew we were there. We sent our canine officers in first, and they flew down the stairs in a blur of fur, barking and gnashing their teeth. They smelled the victims and the blood. We were right behind them with our guns aimed and ready.

Loud yelps pierced the air as the dogs bit into him, but then we heard whining as we rounded the corner because he'd retaliated with his butcher knife, cutting at least one of the dogs. They didn't release their grips on him, though. They were fierce and determined. The K-9 officer whistled to reign them in so we could take over.

"Drop your weapon, Justin, it's over for you!" I bellowed, and Eric ran toward him, ready to fire or chase him down if need be.

"Stop right there, or I'll slice her in two!" he returned, indicating Denise. He was holding the knife to her chest, and her panicked stare was on me.

"It's over, Justin. Give yourself up! You don't want to die like this, but I will kill you if I have to," I ground out between clenched teeth.

He laughed, and it sounded like pure evil if it had a voice. "We made passionate love recently, and now you're threatening to kill me? That's quite the turn of events." The laughter stopped, and his expression grew grave. "If I have to die anyway, what difference does it make? My life is already over. Do you know what it's like to grow up with an abusive father and then be told you have brain cancer? My life was over the day I was born!"

"No, I don't, but you can change your ending. You don't have to waste your entire life like this. You've done so much good in the courtroom, so why this?" I pleaded.

"Because if I don't belong on this earth, no one else does either!" he spat and raised the knife to plunge into my sister.

Before it had the chance to come down on her, though, my gun fired into his head, splattering his brain— the very brain that was killing him. Liam had fired at the same time, striking him in the chest. He immediately crumpled to the cold concrete floor, and one of the dogs scurried over to him to clamp down on his throat.

My hand trembled as I ran to my sister to quiet her sobs while Eric searched the basement for bolt cutters. Marisol searched Justin's body for a key and found it before Eric returned with cutters. While she freed Denise, he worked on Margie Moore, who was sobbing in relief as well. The K-9 officer called for medics, and they were there within minutes. I promised Denise I'd meet her at the hospital. I had to call our parents and give them the wonderful news they'd been longing to hear.

After my emotional phone call, I leaned over Justin's dead body and stared into the face I'd once loved. I would never understand why he had turned into a cold-blooded killer, cancer or not, but I would never regret killing him for it either. Not when it meant saving lives.

I felt a strong hand on my shoulder, and I looked up into Liam's concerned face. "Are you okay?" he asked in a soothing voice.

I shrugged as a tear trickled down. "Just another day at the office, right?"

He slowly nodded. "Sometimes."

As the coroner took Justin away, we headed out of the torture chamber, too, leaving the CSI Unit behind to do their job.

I was glad to hear on the radio that the injured police dog was fine and would fully recover from the stab wound.

As soon as I was on my way to St. Clare hospital, Maria called. "How's my favorite CI?" I greeted her in a chipper voice.

"She's worried about you right now," she replied. "I called to warn you that Carlos Garcia is out on bail, and he wants your blood on his hands."

I knew I should have been worried by the threat, but after the past couple weeks, I just answered with a heavy sigh, "I think he'll have to get in line."

Love this book? Tell Alexis.

Please review on Amazon, GoodReads, or BookBub

Visit Alexis's website:
http://bit.do/AlexisKennedy

- ♥ Leave a comment
- ♥ Watch trailers
- ♥ See what's coming next
- ♥ Check out reviews
- ♥ Check out the blog

Thanks for your continued support!